WARD NURSE

Ward Nurse

by

Helen Sharp

Dales Large Print Books
Long Preston, North Yorkshire,
BD23 4ND, England.

British Library Cataloguing in Publication Data.

Sharp, Helen
    Ward nurse.

    A catalogue record of this book is
    available from the British Library

    ISBN   1-84262-110-6 pbk

First published in Great Britain 1968 by Robert Hale Limited

Copyright   Sharp, Helen, 1

Cover illus   Ward nurse /   rrangement with
P.W.A. Int   Helen Sharp

The moral   LP   asserted

Published   1627769   gement with
Robert Hale Ltd.

Dales Large Print is an imprint of Library Magna Books Ltd.

Printed and bound in Great Britain by
T.J. (International) Ltd., Cornwall, PL28 8RW

CHAPTER ONE

The way Charles Hamilton explained it New Zealanders weren't so much backwards as they simply were unwilling to alter routines and processes which had proved satisfactory for so long.

When Beth Hamilton heard that she dropped a slow wink at Bonnie Harper and took the indulgent wife's tongue-in-cheek attitude without contradicting her husband, for after all no marriage can withstand the small disputes which can so easily be avoided, indefinitely, and Beth Hamilton knew that much about marriage, as well as a good deal more.

'Of course we'll eventually change,' went on Charles, his big, amiable features showing gentle humour up around the blue eyes and down around the long, wide mouth. 'We'll have to. But the trick is of course to try nothing radical until it's no longer radical. Do you follow me, Bonnie?'

The close-cropped curly blonde hair bobbed up and down a time or two. 'Of course, Charles, and I couldn't agree more. Only...'

'Yes; only what?'

'Well,' explained Bonnie lamely, conscious of her sister's soft brown eyes upon her in a critical manner. 'Well; in medicine there are so many revolutionary advances... When one is responsible for the health and the very lives of others...'

Charles waited, then said, 'New Zealand hospitals, I've been told, are as modern as any in the world.'

Beth came to her sister's rescue. 'She didn't mean the hospitals weren't modern, Charles. She only meant they were different. Wasn't that it, Bonnie?'

It wasn't a very good escape but it was better than none so Bonnie nodded, echoing that one word. 'Different...'

It was near supper time. 'High tea' some called it when it was served a bit early, and that had baffled Bonnie too. She wasn't a native and at times she didn't believe she could ever even become an adopted one. She'd learnt her trade in London, had practised it in Australia, Hong Kong, even for one year on an exchange stewardship in New York City, and now she'd been on 'The Small Island' as the Australian seamen had called it on the trip over, three months, and as Beth had said, it was 'different' all right. She wouldn't have used that word; at least she'd not have used it as her sister had. She'd have said things were 'different' in an unflattering way. 'Different' in an old-fashioned, obsolete way.

But Charles was a native. He was the third-generation-Hamilton, of Hamilton and Courtney solicitors. He also happened to be doggedly, almost grimly, pro-New Zealand. Bonnie had just made that discovery. She had also just been saved from an unforgivable *faux pas* by her sister, but then Beth, being five years Bonnie's senior, always had managed to smooth things over. Beth had possessed that rare genius for tactful diplomacy since childhood. Also, she was more placid by nature than Bonnie was. Their parents used to say Beth would cruise through life with a little smile and everyone would smooth out the wrinkles for her, while young Bonnie would fight her way through.

They had been correct.

As Bonnie stood on the verandah outside in the warm night thinking back she could recall dozens of instances when Beth had come along to extricate her from awkward situations. And for Beth it had always seemed so effortless.

Years back Bonnie had admired, even envied, that knack of Beth's. She'd always known exactly when to compromise, what to say and how to say it.

But now, standing on the porch in the warm night Bonnie viewed her sister differently. She'd become too placid, too indulgent, too self-satisfied. She was changed. Or perhaps it was Bonnie who should have changed and who hadn't, who still rebelled against indifference, callousness, what she considered pure ignorance.

It was probably safe to assume that a girl of twenty shouldn't have the same raw edges she'd had at fifteen, particularly since she was so sophisticated in the ways that counted, but Bonnie knew herself well enough to realize that she *hadn't* changed. She thought she was right, too, but there was just enough nagging doubt for her to secretly wonder, and of course all this inner conflict managed to do was to make her miserable.

She hadn't really wanted to visit New Zealand. She'd been to Australia and had believed there wasn't really much difference between the two places. She'd liked Australia; it was backward, yes, but it was full of vigour and confidence; it was shedding its eighteenth-century skin and emerging with a patina of culture and tolerance, industry and commerce, that would have shocked its founders.

But New Zealand wasn't moving along quite so aggressively. In fact it seemed not to be moving ahead at all. The people were excellent; friendly, helpful, generous, but stubborn and hidebound. Bonnie needed no one to tell her when she went to work at the Nicholson Hospital she'd find grim old medical practitioners; she'd found some of that type everywhere she'd been. But what she *hadn't* expected to find was that *every* doctor at Nicholson was of that type.

When she'd made her first recommendation for a simple change, a glowering doctor had told her there were other hospitals over on Campbell Island she might like to work at better. When she'd gone to Doctor Heath who was younger, with a time-saving suggestion, he'd looked into her face sternly and had said, 'Miss Harper there will undoubtedly be things here at Nicholson you'll not quite approve of. That might even be extended to the personnel. But will you please just muffle your dislikes and make a genuine attempt to

11

learn *our* ways instead of re-moulding us all into *your* way?'

She clenched her hands until the nails dug in. That reprimand had hurt worse than all the others combined. She'd admired Doctor Heath, had seen him smile and had heard him laugh. He was a handsome man, pleasant to work around. In fact, being honest with herself, she could have at one time admitted he was more to her than just a professional ideal.

But not after that reprimand. She didn't think it had been fair. It had crushed her because he hadn't been different from the others at all; he'd been just as hidebound, just as reactionary.

Beth came out on to the verandah, lifted her lovely, mature face and watched little lean clouds race across the face of the moon. Without looking at Bonnie she said, 'It's always the same isn't it, love? It's London, New York, Hong Kong – always searching for never-never land where everything is shiny and perfect and efficient.'

She walked up closer, leaned upon the railing beside Bonnie and affectionately regarded the beautiful younger girl. The few years between them seemed actually twice as many. Beth was sturdier, her face plumper, her figure more generous, less lithe and vigorous and high-breasted. She was, as Bonnie had observed, smoothly round, heavy with complacency, not stolid but close to it.

Life had been good to Beth even before well-to-do Charles Hamilton had come round. She'd had the looks, the personality, the smile. Life loved people like Beth; of course back in those days Beth had loved life in return. They had worked out a bland system of reciprocity, each would complement the other. It had worked. Beth had never in her life had to face a genuine crisis. Even when their parents had died she'd already been married and living in the South Pacific. She and Charles had decided to have no children so she'd never had to face the crises in that direction either.

Now, standing beside Bonnie under a yellow moon probably the only dilemma which had ever marred her serene life was Bonnie, and up until a few short weeks back she hadn't had that worry.

'Charles really isn't the best one to discuss New Zealand's backwardness with,' she said. 'I don't see what you compare the place with anyway.'

'New York,' said Bonnie. 'London.'

'Well of course we're just not that large nor wealthy, Bonnie,' said Beth with enduring patience.

The younger woman swung. 'That's exactly the point, Beth, it's not a matter of size nor wealth. It's a matter of simply doing away with procedures which became obsolete after the Second World War.'

Beth sighed, leaned out a little and gazed over where her flowerbeds were. If the soil were loamy one could grow almost anything in New Zealand. Of course among the islands there was a good deal of flinty, rocky soil, but not in the belt of land facing the sea; there, the ground was deep and rich.

Bonnie went to a chair and sat. She had long legs and exquisite ankles. In fact, there were no flaws at all, she was really very lovely. But she didn't look her twenty years. She looked scarcely more than sixteen or seventeen and that had occasioned some inconvenience when she'd had to convince people she was a fully registered and qualified professional nurse.

Beth turned, ran a slow, appraising glance from the ankles up and said, half in fun, 'Bonnie; why don't you just concentrate on finding a husband. That would settle you down.'

With two recent rebuffs – one from Doctor Heath – Bonnie had reason to spit out her reply. 'Men! I wouldn't have one served up on a silver platter, Beth. They are egotistical, pig-headed, dense, self-satisfied and dumb. Plain dumb.'

Beth laughed at the vehemence. 'That handsome Doctor Heath you mentioned last week, love, what of him?'

'A conceited hypocrite!'

Beth's amused eyes slightly widened. 'In just one week?'

'When I told you I thought he was the most handsome man I'd ever seen, I meant it, Beth, but I made a dismal mistake in judging his intelligence. He's as hidebound and old-fashioned as the rest of them at Nicholson.'

Beth gave her head a gentle wag and stood a moment studying her youthful sister. Finally she said, 'Well, please love, don't get Charles upset. All right?'

Bonnie nodded, lifting her face to Beth. 'I'm sorry.'

Beth's smile was soft and tender. 'Little rebel,' she murmured, 'it's late. We really ought to all of us be in bed. Anyway, tomorrow things will look different. Come along.'

Bonnie rose and went over to her sister.

They held hands briefly, each squeezing, then entered the house. They were all that was left of their family. They had always been close and after the death of their parents they became even closer.

But now their lives were pulling them apart, pulling each away to follow her own private star. The memories, the love and understanding and the longing remained, but divergent destinies interfered.

'Charles is already in bed,' whispered Beth, turned and lay a cool palm upon Bonnie's cheek. 'Sleep well, sister. Don't try so hard to change the world. Let someone else carry at least half the load.'

Bonnie smiled and went to her room. Beth was so solid, so good and wise and patient – but she did *not* understand. How could she? Or perhaps it would be better to ask *why* should she? Her world was comfortable, affluent, placid, serene and secure. Why should she care one whit about Nicholson Hospital's antiquated systems!

CHAPTER TWO

Nicholson Hospital was an old building. Not old in the sense of some European hospitals, of course, because New Zealand itself wasn't that old, but the building had been built around the turn of the century and while additions had been stuck on as demand required, very little attention had been paid to its aesthetic appearance.

To Bonnie Harper it looked like a modified prison or one of those oldtime insane asylums. There were actually grilles over the upstairs windows. Worst of all, however, was the sick, pale yellow paint which was re-applied every five or six years. It was a repelling colour and added to the general gloominess of the establishment.

Of course the interior was clean, but only in a rather offhand way. The routines, established perhaps a half or quarter century before were equally as offhanded, and the nurses with the greatest seniority treated everything including one another, as though nothing would or could ever surprise them.

Generally speaking, nothing could, but the attitude of resignation irked Bonnie.

There were no new diseases, perhaps, as she'd been told during her orientation course, but it annoyed her to see how patients were treated. Like so many cattle.

The care was good. It had over the years been refined to such a degree that regardless of the ailment which brought a patient to Nicholson, the nurses had treated dozens of others with the same maladies and knew exactly what to do, and did it. Not with a smile, rarely with a cheery word, never with flowers or music, but with that self-same, demeaning, crisp and monotonous detachment.

There had been a Doctor Chung in Hong Kong – an elfin, wizened man whose lined face and penetrating little black eyes had reflected eternal youth, who had once told Bonnie that in the West doctors treated the body while in the East doctors treated the mind. 'A man can recover from most illnesses, Miss Harper,' Doctor Chung had once smilingly said. 'The body has a great number of self-regulating valves and anti-bodies. The will to live will in many cases bring back health even without medicine. But for a truly successful recovery, concentrate more on the mind. Make a patient smile, lift his spirit, excite his interest, instil in him the conviction that unless he leaves his bed he will miss a fascinating chapter in the continuing story of life. Show him flowers, let him hear music, keep him interested in tomorrow. Always tomorrow.'

She entered her ward wearing a crooked expression. Poor old Doctor Chung, he'd have died a thousand deaths if he'd been transplanted to Nicholson; had to face the demoralizing sameness, the closed, complacent faces she had to work with every day.

The woman in charge of Bonnie's ward was Miss Sampson. The name fitted perfectly. Miss Sampson was in her forties. If there'd ever been any flowing juices in her they'd long ago dried up. She was tall and square with powerful biceps and steel legs. She never laughed and smiled only perfunctorily as though the expression were something to be used only as a rare muscular exercise. She had no imagination but she possessed an acid tongue. Twice Bonnie had felt it and she had no illusions; she'd feel it again.

The ward itself was on the second floor. It was long, wide, with polished linoleum on the floor and dead-white paint on the walls and ceilings. It somehow reminded Bonnie of the below-decks hold of a ship. Of course it had the antiseptic odour usually found in hospital wards.

The beds were ranged neatly along both walls, heads to the wall, feet to the wide aisle. There was a small metal nightstand beside each bed. There were no vases of flowers and while there were wireless sets, they were not generally permitted to be used except in the late afternoon for fear of interrupting the slumber of patients needing their rest.

What was most frustrating to Bonnie was that most of the regulations were valid. Like the radios and flowers. Visitors frequently brought flowers. After dinner they were taken away. The reason was elemental: Pollen tended to aggravate certain maladies.

Candy too, was not generally permitted. Nor were visitors allowed except within specified times. That rule was very strictly enforced. It was over this regulation Bonnie had first got into trouble with Miss Sampson.

An old sheepman with a kidney infection had waited all day for his sons and daughters to visit him. They'd had to drive in from a great distance. Unaware, or perhaps unthinking, they'd arrived after visiting hours. Bonnie had let them in anyway.

Miss Sampson had evicted them and had skinned Bonnie alive for breaking the rules. It didn't matter that the old man's family'd had to come from far out or that they'd had no knowledge of visiting hours. It didn't matter that the old man had lived just for that visit.

'There are no exceptions, Harper,' Miss Sampson had said, standing like Goliath before David, and glaring. 'The doctors themselves cannot break our rules. That's why we have an efficient establishment. You remember that!'

The second infraction had been perhaps more deliberate. The patient, an old woman wasted with abdominal carcinoma, had cherished the six red roses her son had brought. Bonnie had let her hide one rose under her pillow.

That time Miss Sampson had taken Bonnie into her tiny cubicle at the lower end of the ward near the double-hung doors, had told Bonnie to be seated, and had then said, 'Harper; we're hard put to keep qualified nurses. And you are proficient, I'll never take that from you. Except for those things I'd see you sacked this minute. You *knew* better. You've been through our orientation course. You knew those flowers had to go. Now this is your last warning. Short-handed or not we'll tolerate no more infractions.'

Bonnie had sat and looked at the larger, older woman, unable to believe Sampson could really be that heartless. She didn't even begin to get angry until a half hour later, in the cafeteria when she'd been eating with some other girls. Then the anger had come. She'd said, 'It's a prison not a hospital. Sampson's their jailer not their Ward Nurse.'

The other girls had looked embarrassed. Afterwards, most of them avoided Bonnie. The few who still sat in the cafeteria with her at mealtimes, or who strolled in the rose garden out back with her during off-hours, felt somewhat as she did, but they conformed. They even pleaded with her to also conform. Their arguments were similar to that remark Beth had made on the verandah: Let someone else change the world, don't you try it or you'll end up out of work.

The afternoon she met Doctor Fluornoy in the rose garden she'd taken the bit in her teeth. That was three days after the smuggled-rose incident and her anger had died to a slow-smouldering resentment. Doctor Fluornoy was the most prominent surgeon at Nicholson. In fact all he did was surgery. He was a tall, gaunt, grizzled, taciturn man in his mid or late sixties who said little, had a reputation for being testy, and each afternoon took a book of poetry into the rose garden after lunch and read for an hour. The staff called it 'Fluornoy's therapy hour'.

No one interrupted. There were tales of old Fluornoy's temper exploding when anyone at all dared interrupt. Bonnie had heard those tales but that didn't stop her. She saw him sitting in the sunshine with his book. He also had an apple on the bench at his side.

She went over, stopped directly in front of him and waited without saying a word. His grizzled brow creased but he refused to look above the book at her. She didn't move. His cheeks reddened and his mouth drew out flat. She still stood her ground. He finally raised glacial eyes over the book and glared. She smiled.

'I've heard you are angered by interruptions, Doctor Fluornoy, and I don't blame you. Anyone who has had to work at Nicholson thirty years must have long ago lost all empathy.'

The iceberg-blue eyes considered her face, her smile, her fresh beauty without softening. Doctor Fluornoy made only one concession; he lowered his book two inches. 'Get on with it,' he growled. 'What the devil do you want?'

'Nothing. Just to talk.'

'Well go find someone else, young lady.'

'No one else will do, Doctor Fluornoy.'

The book dropped another two inches. He looked her up and down. He sighed and reverently closed the little book, laid it in his lap and composed himself, still bristling with indignation.

'Speak up, girl. Speak up.'

'Have you ever heard of a Doctor Chung in Hong Kong?'

'Not that I recall. And what of him anyway?'

She related the things Doctor Chung had told her. The sun spun a golden web in her close-cropped curly hair. It lay its benign shadings over her perfect features, her violet eyes, her lithe, firm figure. Old Doctor Fluornoy listened without a crack in his craggy features. But there briefly showed an appreciative flicker in the depths of his pale eyes. Any man of sixty-odd, even the hardest and toughest kind of man, could recognize youth and rare beauty, and feel a little sad while beholding it.

When she finished he said, 'Doctor Chung is a wise man, young lady. But where, precisely, does that leave us?'

She then told him of the old sheepman, of the terminal carcinoma case; of the broken visiting rules and the solitary withered red rose.

He blew out a little breath, dropped his hard gaze to the book in his lap and said, 'What is your name?'

'Bonnie Harper.'

'You're in Miss Sampson's ward?'

'Yes, sir.'

The tough eyes lifted again. 'Miss Harper; rules aren't made to be broken. They're made in a place like Nicholson to accommodate the best interests of everyone.' He was being patient. He was, in fact, being almost fatherly. 'I know exactly how you feel. Forty years ago I often felt the same way. But the only way exceptions work in this world is when there are enough individuals like yourself to *make* them work, and here at Nicholson we're already short-handed. Do you understand what I'm saying?'

She didn't say whether she understood nor not. She said, 'Doctor Fluornoy, I'll make the time. I'll do the extra work myself. The woman with the red rose died. She was going to die. She knew it, her son knew it, I knew it. One dried up red rose, Doctor, made it a little easier. That's all I'm saying to you. All I'm pleading for is the little extra service. I'll see to it myself even if it means working over into the next shift.'

He gripped the book in one large, sinewy hand, glanced at his wristwatch and arose. He was considerably taller and looked down into her face. 'Miss Harper; I said I know how you feel. I *do* know. But one nurse setting precedent in a hospital disrupts everything. Good afternoon.'

She didn't let him get away that easily. As he turned to walk off she fell in beside him. She had to extend her stride to keep up.

'Isn't there a compromise?' she asked.

He stopped, looked down and said, 'How old are you?'

'Twenty, sir.'

That seemed to shock him. He patently found it hard to believe she was that old and that she could, at that age, be qualified in her profession. But he recovered quickly

26

and said, 'Miss Harper; life is a compromise. You'll understand that some day. But hospitals are run for efficiency, for disciplined orderliness. They *have* to be run that way. As I just said, one exception ruins the rules and plays hob with morale.'

'Morale?' she exclaimed, stung by his stubbornness. 'Whose morale? I've worked in some of the best hospitals in London and New York and Hong Kong, Doctor. But at Nicholson the morale of the staff comes first when it should be the morale of the patients. The staff is healthy. It's the *patients* who need morale.'

'I see. Doctor Chung speaking,' said old Fluornoy, not without some sarcasm. 'Perhaps the place for you is back in Hong Kong, Miss Harper.'

'No! Doctor Chung doesn't need me but *you do* need me!'

Fluornoy looked a little less patient. 'The idealism of iconoclastic youth, Miss Harper, is hardly new. Rebels without arms seldom achieve much; given enough time any philosophy withers and dies.'

'Doctor; I'm not rebelling against anything. I'm simply trying to do something for people who need something done for them. It's not a new idea.'

27

'No idea is new, Miss Harper, and no pretty girl has yet upset a solid precedent.'

Bonnie's eyes dulled, her shoulders drooped. 'I didn't think you could be this way. They've said you were a great innovator; that you despised routines established to help doctors instead of patients.'

Doctor Fluornoy stood with his light blue gaze upon her face, his features showing no expression. For ten or fifteen seconds he neither spoke nor moved. Whatever his thoughts were she had no idea, but in the end he turned off and walked heavily on into the building with the book of poetry clasped in one hand.

CHAPTER THREE

The following day she was summoned to Doctor Albert Heath's office on the mezzanine. Miss Sampson brought her the message and Sampson's expression was spiteful.

'I've lodged no complaints against you, Harper, but someone evidently has. Good luck.'

She went out into the broad, long hallway

and stood a moment. Doctor Heath was Hospital Administrator. Actually, he was in the process of being re-assigned to ward and examination work after several years as administrator, but he wouldn't assume his new functions for another few days yet. The new man replacing him, Doctor Bryan, was a new intern. He was still struggling to learn all the procedures.

When Bonnie entered the office Bryan looked up, then sprang up. She said her name and that Doctor Heath had sent for her. Bryan didn't speak for a moment but his eyes were lively enough. Eventually he pointed to a second door. 'Through there, Miss Harper – and – when you come out ... luncheon?'

'When I come out, Doctor, I probably won't feel much like luncheon.'

Doctor Heath was waiting. He was a man of average height with soft brown eyes, crinkly blond hair the shade of her own hair, and a wide, humorous mouth that wasn't smiling now. He had some kind of appeal she'd never been able to synthesize, and of course there were millions of men just as handsome, even more so in fact, but somehow, for some reason she couldn't unravel, whenever he was near she could feel his presence in a most pleasant way.

He offered her a chair, sank down on the corner of his desk and looked out the window for a moment before speaking. He was wearing no ward-coat and in shirtsleeves showed powerful chest, shoulders and arms. She guessed he must have been an excellent athlete in college. Then he spoke.

'Why is it new people always have in mind bringing changes? Why can't they simply fit in and quietly go about their work?'

She had an answer ready but didn't use it. She sat with both hands in her lap looking up at him. He *was* the most interesting man she'd ever seen.

He got off the desk, went round it and dropped into the chair back there. 'Miss Harper; I had an unpleasant encounter with Doctor John Fluornoy this morning. It concerned you.'

'I see.'

'I rather imagine you do.' The soft eyes roved over her face and settled briefly upon her lips, then lifted to her eyes. 'Couldn't you have just come to me as you did that other time when you wished to upset things?'

'No sir. You – well – what you said that time hit home.'

'It was meant to hit home, Miss Harper.'

'Was it meant to hurt, Doctor?'

He blinked, 'Hurt?'

Her eyes stung. She jumped up. She hadn't meant to say that and now she was upset. 'Doctor Fluornoy wants me sacked,' she exclaimed fiercely. 'Then get on with it. But don't lecture. I'm not up to taking that this morning.'

Doctor Heath unwound up out of his chair looking a little shocked at her outburst. 'I'm not supposed to fire you,' he said. 'I'm not going to lecture you either. I'm sorry if I've upset you. It was just that sometimes in this job I get so disgusted.' He moved around the desk.

She dug for a handkerchief, the scalding little tears were threatening to gush over and run down her cheeks. She wanted to sink through the floor or run out of the room. The last thing she wanted to do on earth was let this man see her cry. She couldn't find the handkerchief. Doctor Heath offered his, neatly folded, spotless and vaguely fragrant of some after-shave lotion with lavender in it.

She dabbed at her eyes feeling foolish, feeling colour pouring back into her face. She pushed the handkerchief back at him and said, 'If you aren't going to fire me what did you call me in here for?'

He got her chair, moved it up a little and took her arm. 'Please sit down, Miss Harper,' he said in a soft tone of voice. 'I'm awfully sorry.' He looked at her and smiled. 'Better now?'

It was the bedside manner and she recognized it. 'No I'm not better now. Just tell me what I'm doing here and I'll get on back to my ward.'

He recoiled a little from her anger, stood over in front of the desk and said, 'Please, Miss Harper; just let Doctor Fluornoy have his hour of poetry without interrupting.'

'He can have his – damned – hour of poetry,' she flared back. 'And his – damned – hospital too, with its Black Watch nurses and its Torquemadoic surgeons and – and its hideous yellow walls!'

'Yellow walls?'

'Outside walls. Have you ever looked at this place? It looks like a cross between a medieval insane asylum and a – a – slaughter house!'

Doctor Heath stood like stone letting the storm break over him. He offered the handkerchief again and she took it. Finally, he went to the window and gazed downward where he could see the rose garden. He gave her plenty of time to regain full composure. Then he turned and said, 'It is rather ugly, isn't it?' and smiled.

The smile lighted up his whole face. He couldn't have been more than thirty-five but the smile made him appear ten years younger.

'I'd never paid much attention but that is a slightly nauseating colour of yellow.'

She turned suspicious. 'Don't cajole me, Doctor. Here is your handkerchief. Thank you.'

'Keep it,' he said. 'You might need it again.' He walked over to the desk again, leaned upon it and studied her. 'Are you sure you're all right now?'

'Quite sure,' she said icily.

'Well; as a matter of fact Doctor Fluornoy didn't ask me to talk to you. He merely mentioned meeting you in the rose garden yesterday during his reading hour. *I'm* the one who initiated this meeting. The reason I did it was because I recalled having you buttonhole me too, and–'

'I didn't *buttonhole* you, Doctor Heath,' she exclaimed, standing up facing him. 'All I wanted was a moment of your frightfully valuable time. Do you know what you can

33

do with it now – you and John Fluornoy both?'

He looked uneasy but managed a weak smile. 'Quite,' he said. 'You needn't elaborate. But did I ask so very much, Miss Harper? Doctor Fluornoy arrives promptly at six every morning. He works ten, twelve, sometimes fifteen hours every day. That hour in the rose garden...' Doctor Heath's smile firmed up. 'You see?'

'I see! Now would you like my version, Doctor? I'll give it to you anyway! Nicholson is full of fossilized brains, mechanical bodies, drill-sergeant Ward Nurses and scleroid intelligences! All I wanted was to make things a little more humane. And I've committed a terrible crime.'

Albert Heath sighed and gazed at the clock on the wall. 'Miss Harper; would you let me take you to lunch?'

She stopped her tirade, looking at him and said, 'I wouldn't go to lunch with you, Doctor Heath, if you were the only man in the world. I quit!'

'Quit? Miss Harper; could we just forget I ever even asked you to come to the office?'

'We couldn't. And you can tell Doctor Fluornoy–'

The door opened. Doctor Fluornoy

loomed in the opening. He gazed owlishly from Albert Heath to Bonnie Harper and waited for one of them to speak. Neither did so he said, 'Someone wanted to tell Doctor Fluornoy something?'

Bonnie, thrown off by the abrupt appearance of the gaunt older man with his shrewd, hard eyes, didn't have a word left. Doctor Heath offered a sickly smile. 'We were just discussing Nicholson,' he said lamely.

'Yes,' replied Doctor Fluornoy dryly, studying Bonnie's red eyes and cheeks. 'I rather imagine that you were. And its staff. Well; I only wished to stop by and ask, Doctor Heath, when you'd wind up here and be ready to assume your new duties. We can't spend very much more time like this. We are a bit short-handed you know.'

'Tomorrow,' said Heath. 'I'll report to you in the morning, sir.'

Doctor Fluornoy turned his attention back to Bonnie. 'Miss Harper; would you consider giving an old man the pleasure of your company at luncheon in the cafeteria? I promise not to scold you if you'll promise not to try to reform me, make over Nicholson, and put roses beside all the beds.' He didn't give her a chance to answer, but reached, took her arm above the elbow and gently drew her out through the doorway. He then gravely let one eyelid droop at Albert Heath, closed the door and led Bonnie on through the outer office and into the yonder hallway.

'It does an old man good,' he smoothly said, still guiding her along by the arm and giving her no chance to either speak, balk, nor break free, 'to have youth and beauty beside him. And I wasn't really turning down the things you suggested yesterday. But let us go slowly. Let us take a step at a time and not try to run. Do you agree with that?'

He was pacing himself so as not to walk too fast for her. He was speaking smoothly, the way a doctor speaks to a frightened patient. It was quite different from the way he'd spoken to her the day before.

She said, 'Doctor, you don't have to humour me. You don't have to pretend you didn't disagree with me yesterday and that you couldn't care less right now about the things I suggested. I have quit. I told Doctor Heath that, so perhaps as one of his last acts as administrator will be to take care of the termination forms for me.'

They started down the ramp into the

subterranean hospital restaurant, built into what may have once been designed as a huge storage area or a bomb shelter, but in either case it was quite large and unimaginatively painted the same colour as the outside of the building.

Doctor Fluornoy nodded to a pair of nurses leaving the restaurant. A portly doctor stopped him for a brief question and a gangling youthful intern gawked at old Doctor Fluornoy escorting a gorgeous young nurse. About that he said in a quiet voice, 'Ah-hah; you have just seen how gossip is born. The look in that young man's eyes was conception. Upstairs, wherever he works, will be the area of delivery. By tonight all Nicholson will have heard the old curmudgeon, John Fluornoy is courting a very handsome young lady.'

They went to a table which obviously was reserved for him. The other tables close by were taken, people chatted, ate, and surreptitiously watched old Fluornoy gallantly hold a chair for his guest.

To Bonnie it was all very pleasant, now that her anger and exasperation had diminished. In fact she could almost smile over the very deliberate gallantry of Doctor Fluornoy. But she was firm about one thing:

She was going to leave Nicholson Hospital.

They ordered, then Doctor Fluornoy leaned his forearms upon the table, made a leisurely study of her face and said, without smiling, he thought she wasn't quite the gladiator he'd considered her the day before.

'I was rather impressed yesterday. Well; not terribly impressed *favourably*, you understand. After all you did deprive me of my moment of pleasure. But I'll give the devil his due; you had spunk to brace me like that, and you had very noble ideas.'

She cut through this somewhat rambling dissertation. 'Doctor; I resigned in Albert Heath's office fifteen minutes ago. Whatever you thought of me yesterday or whatever you think of me right now, doesn't concern me.'

'Come, come,' he said. 'Prove to yourself if not to me that you *are* a gladiator.'

'A gladiator...?'

'Don't give up, Miss Harper. Don't surrender simply because you've run into a bit of adversity. Stay and wage your campaign until the last bitter shot. In other words, prove to yourself that you are capable of supporting your personal convictions.'

Bonnie waited until their meal was served then gazed straight into the steely old eyes to say, 'Doctor Fluornoy; could it be that you are a hypocrite; that you know very well Nicholson is critically short-handed?'

He didn't smile but he inclined his head a little while studying his turtle soup. 'It's possible, Miss Harper.' Then he looked straight at her. 'Wouldn't you be interested in knowing which?'

She slowly smiled. She understood this hard, dedicated, no-nonsense old man. 'Tell me one thing, Doctor; do you honestly believe, if I were to remain at Nicholson and were to continue my fight, there would be a possibility that someday I might force some changes in procedures and routines?'

'A very strong possibility,' he murmured, dipping into his soup. 'A very strong possibility indeed. But don't expect me to be an ally. You'll have to do this all alone.' He paused between spoonfuls. 'Well...?'

'I'll stay, Doctor.'

'I knew you would. Now suppose we get on with our meal. I've three surgeries this afternoon.'

CHAPTER FOUR

The forthcoming half hour was going to be dismally unpleasant and Albert Heath knew it. Whenever Doctor Fluornoy, Nicholson Hospital's chief surgeon sauntered into an office with his ward-coat unbuttoned and took a chair, someone was going to get raked up one side and down the other. Old Fluornoy did not waste time. He was not constituted for idle persiflage. Heath happened to know too, that Doctor Fluornoy'd handled three surgeries the afternoon before, right after he'd taken Bonnie Harper to lunch, and that today his schedule was no less stringent.

'My boy,' said old Fluornoy gruffly but kindly, 'the young lady is very lovely. She is also very spirited. Now as a young man, I used to make quite a study of young ladies, and while I've aged somewhat, young ladies as such have not materially altered.'

Up to that point in the one-sided conversation Doctor Fluornoy's voice had remained amiable, garrulous, rambling.

Now it changed. It crackled and snapped.

'Any fool, Heath, could have seen Miss Harper was upset when she entered this office yesterday. Anyone but a bumbling simpleton would realize she is very efficient at her work and that Nicholson is critically short-handed as it is without you acting the utter ninny and goading her into resigning. Only a damned pipsqueak would have made a mountain out of such a molehill; when we discussed her interrupting my garden-hour it was not to convey to you some idea you had to become Sir Galahad and save me from Miss Harper.'

Albert Heath took the tongue-lashing the same way he'd taken Bonnie's fury the day previous; he remained obdurate and silent, waiting for the thunderheads to roll past. Finally he said, 'Doctor Fluornoy, I didn't have any idea she'd quit.'

'Then you're a fool,' growled the older man. 'Look at her, Heath: she has great spirit.'

'And I didn't really rebuke her, sir. All I did was—'

'I don't give a damn what you did, Heath. I'm only interested in what it caused. I'm out of pocket for a luncheon and I'm out of sorts with your bungling. I managed to

41

cajole her into staying on, but good lord man if you don't develop some tact we'll lose the lot of 'em.'

'Yes, sir,' said Doctor Heath a trifle stiffly.

Old Fluornoy arose, stood hunched at the shoulders with both hands shoved deep into his pockets and continued wearing that critical expression as he studied the younger man. Eventually he asked a question which was quite out of context. 'You are un-married are you not, Doctor?'

'Yes sir.'

Fluornoy didn't enlarge on that. He turned towards the door, opened it and looked back to say, 'I'll expect you in Ward B this afternoon. If I'm not there promptly when you arrive, please ask Ward Nurse Sampson to orientate you. Ward B will be part of the new itinerary.'

Fluornoy left, Doctor Heath dolorously wagged his head, waited until he was certain Fluornoy was beyond his front office, then went over and poked his head out. Doctor Bryan was leaning back smiling at the ceiling. Heath barked at him.

'If you've run out of work, Mister Bryan, I'll look up some more for you!'

Young Bryan's chair came down with a crash as he dived for his mail basket.

Perhaps he reflected, and perhaps he did not reflect upon it, but there was one indisputable truth concerning chains of command; no matter who got roasted by a superior, there was always a subordinate he could roast in turn.

Ward Nurse Sampson hadn't been in the restaurant simultaneously with Harper and Doctor Fluornoy but she'd heard of them having lunch together within fifteen minutes of it happening. Still, she had nothing to say to Bonnie that afternoon. She restrained herself until the following day, and even then, although consumed by avid curiosity, because she and Bonnie were existing in a vacuum, she merely asked if Doctor Heath had sacked her.

Since the answer was obvious – Bonnie was still there, wasn't she? – the only satisfaction Sampson got was a very sweet, girlish smile and not one word by way of explanation.

In the afternoon when Doctor Heath appeared at Sampson's tiny Ward Office, after she'd shown him all the reports and charts on patients in Ward B, she said, 'I hardly expected Harper to be on the job this morning, Doctor.' It was an excellent opening for Doctor Heath but he didn't take it. His expression clouded with unpleasantness and he grunted. That was all.

Sampson was then convinced that somehow – she was totally at a loss to imagine such a thing actually happening – Harper had got the best of both Heath and Fluornoy. It was, to say the very least, an incredible circumstance. On the other hand, within the purview of Sampson's logic, she could understand one thing very easily: Harper was very attractive. Heath and old Fluornoy were men. Sampson was indignant about the reasonable conclusion she drew from those things. She also decided that because Harper could wrap two foolish males around her lovely little finger, Harper would certainly find out no such strategy would work with the head nurse of Ward B!

As Doctor Heath made his initial tour of the ward he inevitably encountered Bonnie. Where they met was at the bedside of an elderly Basque sheepman, a leathery, silent, wizened man with eyes the colour of wet obsidian and hair to match despite his moderately advanced age. The Basque and Bonnie were friends. He had no family and although he had friends in the back-country, he had none in any of the coastal cities. In fact, as he explained in accented English, in forty years he'd only visited the cities when he'd been compelled to, as now, when illness had forced him down out of the lonely hills.

She was concerned for his flock but he reassured her the second day after his admittance; there were other sheepmen who'd take care of his camp until he returned. He'd then said, with a wry twinkle, 'And if I don't come back they will divide everything. That is the way it is done.'

The Basque, however, would only nod at Doctor Heath. Even when he was asked questions he declined to answer aloud. He'd nod or wag his head but he wouldn't speak aloud.

But Doctor Heath was no novice; he didn't insist on verbal answers as he made his examination and studied the chart upon the foot of the bed. Later, taking Bonnie away by the arm, he said, 'Nothing very serious. The so-called wonder drugs will clear up his infection. But I've often wondered how many of those people die and are buried in the out-back simply because they will not come to the city for treatment.'

She knew, from the old Basque, something

about that. 'After he gets to trust you, Doctor, he'll talk. And he's awfully interesting.'

'I imagine he is. Those people very often develop a philosophy all their own.'

'He has one,' she said. 'He told me that a man's life isn't important.'

Heath's eyebrows shot up. 'He could get some argument there.'

She seemed about to say more but after his tart comment she didn't. Instead she turned professional. 'Do you wish me to go along with you, Doctor?'

Looking at her, his lips drooped. 'I did it again, didn't I, Miss Harper? I've got a knack for it.'

'For what, Doctor?'

'Stepping on your toes.'

He turned and went back over to the beds. She watched him a moment, a shadow in her gaze, then Sampson beckoned and she hastened to the lower end of the ward.

There were two fresh patients to be docketed in and put to bed. It was all routine; the patients stood in bathrobes, both men, both diffident and shorn of all dignity by the meat-grinder efficiency of Nicholson's admittance procedure. Bonnie smiled at them trying to make them feel like individuals again. Sampson saw that and scowled as she barked questions and scribbled down the answers.

Neither of the new admittees were seriously ill; one had high blood pressure, the other had a fused disc in the spine. He'd had surgery once but evidently the demoralizing and persistent ache in the back hadn't been alleviated.

Bonnie took them to the beds assigned by Sampson then returned for their charts. Sampson was waiting with a cool comment. 'It's not necessary to make them feel so much at home; this isn't the Crown Hotel you know.'

Bonnie took the charts, held them a moment while she gazed at the older woman. Finally she said, 'Did you know it takes less muscular effort to smile than to scowl, Miss Sampson?' and walked off.

Doctor Heath finished in Ward B and left. He was required to tell Sampson where he'd be but since she wasn't at the Ward Office when Heath entered it, and Bonnie was there, he told her.

'Going down to Examinations for a bit, Miss Harper. After that I'll be upstairs in Surgery for a conference with Doctor Fluornoy.'

She nodded and for a moment they stood

gazing at each other. Then he left and she was summoned by a buzzer to one of the patients. She did not see Albert Heath the balance of that day although, later in the afternoon Sampson sent for him to look at a patient in the ward.

When she had a free moment she went down to the rose garden. Doctor Fluornoy wasn't there. He had been, but his 'therapy hour' had passed and he was back on the third floor again.

Two other nurses she knew were sitting smoking. It wasn't permitted in the building. Sampson, an aggressive non-smoker, had asked first off whether or not Bonnie smoked. Sampson took smoking among the nurses and patients as a personal affront. All it took to get Sampson to launch into a statistical harangue about the perils of tobacco was one small question, or a whiff of smoke.

The nurses who sat with Bonnie in the garden had both served under Sampson and when they sat down asked Bonnie how she was standing up under it. She didn't mention quitting the day before and in fact she was rather charitable towards the Ward Nurse, although she certainly didn't feel that way.

It was one of those routine days. Nothing very unusual occurred, time dragged a bit, and along towards five o'clock Bonnie's arches ached slightly, which was not at all unusual in her vocation. It had been repeatedly stated, in training and afterwards, that varicose veins and ruined feet were the prices one had to pay to make a career of nursing.

But what was infinitely worse was the boredom caused by restrictions. It was basically this boredom which occasionally caused rebellion among nurses. But after five or ten years most nurses simply gave in, became domesticated to the mindless routines, and perhaps after they'd been at it as long as Sampson, they took refuge in the mindlessness.

Bonnie hadn't reached either the first nor second phases yet. She proved it the very next day by sneaking half a glass of red wine to the Basque. He was very grateful; it was the custom among his people, he told her, to drink red wine with their meals. They also drank it during the heat of each summer day. It was better for the body, he informed her gravely, than too much water. Furthermore it was a tonic; people who drank only water had soft muscles. Those who drank sparingly of wine turned into pure sinew and rawhide. Men who had been raised on red wine lived to be very old, and were useful every day of their lives.

She neither believed him nor entirely disbelieved him. She had her own explanation: Environment. She didn't attempt to explain this to the sheepman however. She was more concerned with whisking away the tell-tale glass after he'd finished with it.

The patient with the fused disc was slated for additional corrective surgery although he told her somewhat fearfully it would do no good; that once a man's back gave out he would suffer for the rest of his life. She didn't argue, instead she brought two books from the downstairs medical library, both having to do with fusions.

The following day Doctor Heath told her he thought the Basque would be able to get up and go sit in the garden within another day or two. He also told her the man slated for back-surgery was more cheerful than he'd been the day before.

'Must have had a good night's rest, or else a pleasant dream.'

She said sweetly, 'Or a little sympathetic care, Doctor Heath,' and left him to go down where Sampson was beckoning.

He stood pondering her remark and watching her for a moment, then turned and glanced first at the Basque, then at the surgical patient. He had the makings of a good physician and surgeon, primarily because he was thoughtful, observant, and shrewd. He sauntered over to the bed of the man with the fused discs to make quiet conversation. He didn't go to the Basque because he knew he'd get no answers there.

CHAPTER FIVE

The following week when the moon was full, the evening warm, and dinner was finished at the Hamilton residence, Bonnie and Beth went out upon the verandah while Beth's husband retired to his study to labour over some legal briefs.

It was one of those quiet, languid nights. Everything could happen or nothing at all could happen. There was a silence roundabout, the city lay below spread out like a tumbled pearl necklace, lights rising from the plain near the sea all the way up the mountainsides parallel and even higher, than the Hamilton home.

Fragrance from sea and land, from flowers and trees, made the air heavy and cloying. It put Bonnie in mind of other places in the South Pacific. Raratonga, the nameless little fly-speck islands lying like giant steps from Hawaii to Japan, flower covered, densely forested, lush green and limpid. She said something about this to Beth, but except for a hurried honeymoon years before her sister had visited none of those places. She simply replied by saying New Zealand, with all its drawbacks, was a civilized paradise and she loved it.

Bonnie could understand that; Beth throve on serenity. Most women did. If there was one thing women shunned it was innovation, struggle, strife of any kind. Bonnie was different. Or else she was simply very young at heart.

She said, referring to the fact Beth had insisted Bonnie live with them, 'I think it would be better, Beth, if I got a room nearer Nicholson. Somewhere closer to the city.'

Her sister gazed across through the silvery moonlight. 'Just to be nearer the hospital, or because you're a little out of things up here in the residential area?'

Bonnie couldn't answer it like that, and it

had nothing to do with living above and beyond the city. 'Not the hospital,' she replied, watching the blinking high lights of a large aircraft swinging in from mainland Asia. 'In fact I've been thinking of giving up nursing. Perhaps find something down in the city where someone might welcome a little creativity.'

Beth stared. 'Leave nursing, Bonnie. Why, ever since you were a child – fifteen or sixteen – you've had your heart on nursing as a profession.'

'If I'd known then what I know now I'd have tried for a medical degree.'

'You're restless, love. It's that time of year.'

An auto was creeping up towards them. Its lamps had first been noticeable where it had left the central roadway to begin the climb. Bonnie was watching it make a creeping ascent as though the driver were unfamiliar with his whereabouts.

'Restless or not,' she said a trifle tartly, 'Nicholson has about brought me to heel, Beth. It's – well – it's too stifling. I do what I can but what can one nurse do?'

'I should imagine quite a lot, really.'

'I thought so too, once, but as the weeks rolled by I saw that all I was accomplishing was to make things easier for a few people in

Ward B, while in the other wards nothing had changed.'

'Isn't Nicholson an excellent institution?' asked Beth, not really troubled but interested. 'I've always heard it's one of the best.'

Bonnie, still watching the approaching auto, made a little unladylike snort. 'That would depend upon what you compared it with. I should think in comparison to Dachau or Treblinka it would appear a fine hospital. But compared to ... Beth? That car is coming here. Were you expecting anyone?'

Beth looked. 'Perhaps Charles was, I certainly wasn't or I wouldn't be sitting out here in slippers. I'd better at least put on shoes.' Beth arose but made no immediate move to leave. 'I'm sure I don't recognize the car,' she said, as the vehicle paused out front, then crawled close to the kerbing and stopped with a little lurch. It was a small car but not of the mini-variety. It shone too, as though it wasn't very old, and that wasn't common either in New Zealand where the import duty on autos was murderous.

'No,' whispered Bonnie, stiffening in her chair as the driver climbed out, stepped round front and started resolutely up towards the house. 'It's Doctor Heath!'

Beth, looking swiftly at her sister because

of the odd tone of voice she'd used when she'd recognized the newcomer, turned back and made a very close and deliberate appraisal of the husky man striding forward. She'd heard enough – sometimes almost ecstatic, sometimes downright condemnatory – to be intrigued.

Bonnie arose. 'Good evening,' she said coolly as Heath stepped upon the first step. 'Are you lost, Doctor Heath?'

He peered into the verandah's steady gloom and smiled. Beth thought it a handsome smile. In fact, when he stopped in moonlight where she could catch a good glimpse, she thought he was indeed quite handsome.

'Not now I'm not,' he said lightly. 'I've never been up here before. This is where the swells live. I'm only a working peasant.'

Beth went forward to introduce herself. Albert Heath took the last two steps in one easy stride and took her extended hand, smiling down at her. 'I've heard of your husband,' he said easily, and charmed Beth all the way to a chair.

Bonnie stood her ground without speaking. She had a premonition. She was positive of one thing; Albert Heath hadn't hunted her down unannounced just to pass the time of evening. She waited for him to stop charming Beth. It wasn't a very long wait. Beth retreated into the house, whether to simply put shoes on or to tell her husband they had a guest, Bonnie didn't know – nor care. She stood in the silvery shadows waiting.

He turned, stepped closer and eased down upon the verandah railing. He was tieless and instead of a jacket wore a light cardigan sweater. He smelt of that lavender aftershave lotion she'd first noticed on his handkerchief, and appeared both relaxed, and somehow, even in the shadows, somewhat weary. But he kept smiling.

'You're on guard,' he told her. 'I don't blame you. I'm not exactly your idea of the perfect friend, am I?'

'You drove a long way to ask me that, Doctor,' she said, still standing.

He shook his head slightly at her. 'Won't you sit down? Just this once can't we talk without innuendos?'

She remained standing and said nothing. She had no intention of making this easy for him. She knew it was too late for him to invite her to go to dinner with him, moreover he wasn't dressed for it.

He lost his little smile. 'All right, Miss

Harper. I've some bad news for you and drove up to deliver it personally.'

'Yes of course,' she murmured. 'You wouldn't want to let that opportunity slip by would you?'

He was quiet for a moment, regarding her, then shrugged so slightly she almost didn't see it. 'It's not exactly bad news, in a way. In another way… Well; Miss Sampson had an accident. She was struck by an auto.'

Bonnie sat down. 'Bad…?'

'Bad enough I'm afraid. Broken ribs, bruises … I left before the examination had been completed.'

'You rushed here to tell me…?'

'Yes. But not out of charity I'm afraid. You see, you'll have to take over as Ward Nurse until Sampson's back on her feet. We'll want you to report in tomorrow morning at six instead of eight o'clock. Do you mind awfully? I realize it's a shock.'

She continued looking at him. A shock? It was stunning. It fairly took her breath away. 'There must be more qualified nurses, Doctor Heath.'

'You know how frightfully short-handed we are, Miss Harper. The others wouldn't know Ward B routines.'

'Is this your idea?'

'Yes. But I cleared it through Doctor Fluornoy. He was favourable.'

'I don't know,' said Bonnie, leaning gingerly back in the chair. 'We have fifty patients, Doctor.'

'You are familiar with each case.'

'Yes, but I'm not familiar with the records system except in a very cursory manner, nor with the procedures Miss Sampson has set up in her office.'

'You'll have all the help I can get you. The issue isn't really routines so much as it is the need – the *imperative* need – for a Ward Nurse to be in charge. After all we can't just have Ward B nurses wandering around, can we?'

Beth returned with her heels on. She'd also changed from the little rumpled house dress into something a little more presentable. And she'd brushed her lovely, wavy hair until it shone in the moonlight.

Doctor Heath arose as she came on to the verandah. She smiled at his gallantry and asked him to have a chair. He sat back down on the railing, explained to Beth why he was there and enlisted her as an ally in persuading Bonnie.

Actually, it wasn't simply that Bonnie was lacking in confidence, it was also her deep-down knowledge that she'd never run Ward B – or any other ward – the way Sampson did. And if that didn't get her into trouble with the other members of staff, including Heath and John Fluornoy, it most certainly would ensure her trouble with Sampson when the Head Nurse recovered sufficiently to take back over again.

She heard her sister and Albert Heath talking quietly to one side of her. She could tell by the tone of Beth's voice that she was pleased with Doctor Heath. For no reason she could have analysed right then, Bonnie said, 'I'm sorry, Doctor. I'll take over in one of the other wards so that you can transfer some other Ward Nurse.'

He turned away from Beth and sat for a while just gazing at her. Then he arose and without being able to see it in his face Bonnie knew he was angry. She looked at him closely; she'd never seen him angry before.

'I thought,' he said, enunciating very clearly, 'you wanted responsibility. That's why I took the time to drive up here tonight, Miss Harper. I thought you wanted to create, to innovate. I had no idea that was just all talk.'

He turned his back to her and stepped to

the edge of the verandah, murmured something quiet to Beth and started down the
steps. Bonnie let him get all the way to the
bottom before she arose and said, 'Doctor;
anyone receiving the news you brought
would be stunned. And I'll admit to having
shaky confidence in myself right at this
minute. But the main reason I won't
become Head Nurse in Ward B is because of
what would happen the moment I changed
anything. And I wouldn't take the job even
temporarily *without* making some changes.'

His exasperation was visible out in the
moonlight. He threw out both arms. 'You
were going to quit last week weren't you?
Then what worse thing could happen now?
Nothing, except that you'd be permitted to
resign, and meanwhile you'd have Ward B
for your damned guinea pig.' He dropped
both arms and gazed up at her. 'I don't
understand you, Miss Harper. This is the
chance you've needed and I came up here to
personally hand it to you – then you turn
tail and hide your head.'

She went to the steps and down them. He
had reasoned the thing out correctly and
she knew it. What *was* the worst thing that
could happen; she'd have to resign when
Sampson came back on duty and Nichol-

son's staff vetoed her innovations. Well; she'd just been telling Beth she thought she'd chuck it all anyway.

'Doctor, thank you for coming up. I apologize for being such a boor. Of course I'll take over until Miss Sampson is back on her feet.'

He startled Bonnie and shocked her sister, back there on the porch; he took one step forward, laid both hands upon Bonnie's shoulders – and kissed her. Then, while the shock still held both women stock-still, he stepped back widely smiling.

'You've just salvaged my pride, Miss Harper. You see, Doctor Fluornoy said if I couldn't get you to take over, I'd have to, and in case you didn't know it, there is nothing more degrading to an up-and-coming practising physician than to be demoted to the capacity of Ward Nurse. I'll see you in Ward B at six in the morning.' He turned and ran to his car, meshed gears and proceeded to back around to head back down the way he'd come.

Beth said, 'Well; he certainly didn't impress me as the impetuous kind – at first.'

Bonnie, returning to her chair, smiled at her sister. 'I didn't think he knew how. You should see him at the hospital; the model of professional propriety.' Bonnie held a hand to her lips briefly, watching thin clouds scud over the face of the moon before she spoke again.

'Do you suppose that being Ward Nurse working with him, and being decidedly sly about it, I could manoeuvre him into a consultation on cases over supper in the city, Beth?'

The older woman's placid, handsome features brightened a little. 'If you couldn't, love, believe me no other girl could. There's not another one on the island who could compare with you for outright beauty.'

'He smelled good,' murmured Bonnie, and leaned back to continue watching the diaphanous clouds cross in front of the ancient moon.

CHAPTER SIX

The extent of Sampson's injuries weren't much more serious than Doctor Heath had initially reported to Bonnie. He'd said there were broken ribs and bruises, which there were, but he'd left the examination room where Sampson was undergoing preliminary treatment before an X-ray showed a fractured arm and wrist.

Fortunately for Sampson she was one of those muscular, rugged individuals. She had the constitution of a horse. By the time she'd been sedated and bandaged she had a good round curse for the driver who'd struck her down.

Bonnie was too busy as Ward Nurse to look in on Sampson until later that first day, which was just as well for Sampson needed rest more than she needed visitors.

Albert Heath'd had Sampson put across the wide corridor in Ward A. He didn't explain why he'd done that and Bonnie didn't ask, but they both knew very well why he'd done it. Of course, after a few days, Sampson would understand too.

In order for Bonnie to arrive at Nicholson at six in the morning she had to arise at four-thirty. It was a wretched time to be getting out of bed. What kept it from being entirely horrible was the fact that this was summer, the dawns were warmly exquisite, and she'd been excited.

Every other nurse was on duty when she arrived, so after making certain breakfast was on the way up for the patients, and seeing to it that the girls were caring for the patients, washing them, she accepted Albert Heath's invitation to step into the staff room across the hall for coffee.

'It won't be so bad,' he told her. 'The main thing is to feel your way slowly the first day or two.'

'It's lack of confidence,' she confided. 'It just came too suddenly.'

He smiled. 'That's what Sampson said about the automobile that struck her down.'

'There isn't any danger of internal injury is there?'

'With Sampson? She has no intestines, Bonnie, didn't you know that: she has a cast-iron heart, a steel spine, analine blood and a computer mind. She'll be all right. But it'll take at least two months. One thing Sampson isn't, is young. She's not going to spring from bed and run anyone a foot-race for a while.'

She learned something interesting that first day as Ward Nurse: when in doubt never let others know it. She'd give orders to her nurses with a trembling heart. They'd march off to carry them out perfectly satisfied, because she *showed* no fear, that she knew exactly what she was about.

That afternoon she received a lovely

bouquet from the Basque. He'd been discharged two days previous. The card said he would always remember her. That helped pull her through.

Albert Heath was called away in mid-afternoon but by then she was sure she'd be able to cope with anything that came up. Actually, this first day, she merely kept things going as smoothly as possible without changing anything. She did that the second and third days also. It took that long for the feeling of confidence to come. On the fourth day she received three young girls, sisters, who'd been seriously injured in an auto accident. They occupied all her time. On the fifth day a minor crisis had to be resolved, and therefore she did nothing startling the first week as Head Nurse.

But the following Monday after she'd received her cheque, she made one change in the routine. She had a newsboy go through the ward distributing the daily paper. The patients were delighted and for an hour afterwards except for the rattling of turning pages, the ward was as quiet as could be.

On Tuesday she had the three sisters moved closer to her tiny office, then had an isolation curtain put up which screened them off. They were brought flowers and an extra dish of ice-cream. When she could she went in and sat with them. One was very lovely – except for twenty-one stitches above the temple where her hair'd been shaved away. She fretted and wept until Bonnie showed her how by wearing her hair differently, she'd be able to conceal the scar.

Doctor Heath, serious at first over the condition of the girls, told Bonnie over in the staff room near the end of the second week, he'd witnessed few such swift recoveries; that he'd anticipated all manner of psychological problems. 'Whenever pretty girls are hurt, especially in the visible areas, they go through all manner of mental suffering. I dread that much more than patching them up.'

Towards the end of the second week Bonnie inaugurated a minor revolution that brought a great growl from Doctor Fluornoy. She told each patient exactly what their trouble was and for those who expressed interest she had books sent up to Ward B from the downstairs medical library.

The first repercussion came the following Tuesday when a man with a kidney ailment got into a technical argument with one of the male laboratory technicians. The following day a bull-necked longshoreman with a broken collarbone and in need of corrective surgery, had the temerity to challenge Doctor Fluornoy as he was being wheeled into surgery. That's how it came to be known that the patients in Ward B had all become amateur doctors. When Fluornoy met Albert Heath in the cafeteria that day he started out by saying, 'What in the merry hell are you trying to do down there, Heath? I had a surgery case who chose to dispute my method of going on. I've asked round and it seems you've depleted the medical library.'

Doctor Heath smiled a trifle weakly. 'Ward Nurse Harper,' he murmured. 'Do you recall her, Doctor Fluornoy?'

Of course the older man recalled Bonnie, but just for a moment he stood in thought before understanding the innuendo behind Heath's words. Then he puckered his brow. 'Yes, of course. Extremely beautiful girl. She's in charge now, what? Heath; that was *her* idea, educating patients concerning their ailments?'

'It most certainly wasn't mine, Doctor.'

'I see. And what other devilment's she been up to?'

'Well, really nothing. What I mean, Doctor Fluornoy, is that while she's made some changes, they've all been quite beneficial and haven't interfered with–'

'I'll be down and see for myself when I have an opportunity,' said old Fluornoy, scowling at Albert Heath. 'Since when have you become a bumbling dissembler, Heath; you're stumbling around with words today.'

Doctor Heath hastened back to Ward B to tell Bonnie of his encounter with John Fluornoy. He found her neither lacking in confidence nor unprepared. As she told him, people don't grasp opportunities without realizing there may be adverse reactions.

Heath was dubious but he didn't say so; in fact he never said so, yet he managed to keep rather busy in the ward for the balance of the day so as to be on hand when John Fluornoy arrived.

He didn't arrive. Not that day nor the next day, and on the day after that it wouldn't have done him any good to appear because Ward Nurse Harper went into the city in the afternoon and did not reappear in her domain until the night shift had taken over. She had a long talk with the Night Ward Nurse which ended with scarcely restrained girlish laughter, then she went home.

That night Albert Heath came calling again, this time wearing a coat, a necktie, and bearing a golden gardenia in a little box which he called his 'peace offering' although they'd been getting along splendidly lately. He took her to dinner down in the city.

She wore a dark dress with a tiny diamond clasp upon the right shoulder, no other jewellery, and carried a black coat. Dark always set her fair colouring off to perfection. She knew it, and when they alighted in front of the restaurant uptown, *she* knew *he* knew it.

It was the first time since she'd arrived in New Zealand she'd actually been out to dinner. When she told him that she had to also explain that her sister and brother-in-law had asked her to go along several times but she'd just never felt much like it.

He said, 'Hardly much challenge in going to supper with a sister and brother-in-law, eh?'

She didn't answer but arched her brows and gazed steadily at him. He blushed, held up the menu and became quite busy.

When their meal came he explained that as a bachelor he ate here often, that he liked it above just about every other café in the city, and when a striking long-legged girl with dark red hair sauntered past and deliberately dropped him a wink so that Bonnie would see it, he said his friends also ate here.

She had to bite her lip to keep from laughing at his acute discomfort.

He recounted for the second time his discussion with Doctor Fluornoy in the hospital cafeteria. She shrugged it off. 'Remember what you told me, Doctor? I was going to quit anyway; what's the worst that could happen? If Doctor Fluornoy comes in like a bull elephant I'll hand *him* the job as Head Nurse, Ward B.'

Heath smiled. It wasn't an altogether delighted smile. Bonnie turned once to exchange a long, cool glance with the beautiful redhead. They took each other's measure and if the redhead was older by a few years and more sophisticated in dress and cosmetics, Bonnie had the poise and self-assurance to match. It was a stand-off so both girls broke off and turned back to their companions.

'He'll die if he shows up tomorrow afternoon,' she said to Albert Heath as though there'd been no little interlude with the ravishing redhead.

He looked mildly puzzled. 'Who; Doctor Fluornoy?'

She didn't answer the question. 'The painters will arrive tonight and be finished by morning. It cost a bit more that way but they understood.'

Heath sat blankly, 'They did?'

'Yes. Too much traffic through Ward B during daytime. None at all to speak of at night. And anyway it'll give the place time to air out, to lose the paint fumes.'

'Sure,' he murmured. 'Of course... What paint fumes?'

'Didn't I tell you, Doctor,' she said sweetly. 'I hired a crew of painters to redecorate Ward B.'

'...You *what!*'

'A warm very light tan with darker tan for trim. That way there'll be no sunglare in the afternoon and otherwise it'll be a very restful atmosphere.' She kept that girlish smile and leaned upon the table. There was a high, creamy cleavage the way she was leaning and he dropped his eyes once, then jumped them back to her face with rust in his cheeks. He put aside his napkin and said, 'Bonnie; you just can't unilaterally decide to redecorate Ward B. There is a governing body that establishes all hospital policy.'

'I am quite aware of that, Doctor. Even the Americans use that same system.'

'You didn't submit the idea of redecorating the ward...?'

71

She softly shook her head. 'You know I didn't, Doctor.'

He sagged slightly. 'Yes, I did. At least I *should* have known.' He pulled himself together and frowned. 'You're trying awfully hard to be sacked, love. Old Fluornoy'll go off like a sky-rocket.'

She shrugged. 'Then let him sack me. The ward will be redecorated and as tight-fisted as the governing board appears to be, at least they won't do the ward over again – so I'll have at least accomplished that much.'

'Bonnie,' he said very seriously. 'Why didn't you at least wait until the shock of the library incident died down a bit?'

'Doctor; I once read something Napoleon said. When you decide to attack hit hard, hit fast, and keep on hitting; never permit your adversary to recover from a defensive posture.'

He groaned, signalled for a re-fill of their coffee cups and looked morose. 'Fine,' he grumped. 'Only you're not Napoleon. You're not even Joan of Arc.'

The coffee came. She didn't touch hers but he absently stirred his. She cocked her head at him. 'Albert.' It was the first time she'd used his first name but right then he didn't seem to realize that. 'Albert. *I'm* the one in hot water. Not you. And something you said made me decide to do what I've done. It's changed my entire philosophy towards the job: the worst that can happen is that I'll be sacked.'

She watched him drink the coffee and put the cup aside. He was very good looking, but she'd privately made that observation before. He did something to her. She'd had that feeling before too. She kept leaning on the table until he said perhaps they'd ought to get on back to their respective homes.

She let him place the coat over her shoulders but as they turned to depart she turned slowly, deliberately, for one last confrontation with the luscious redhead. She gave the older, more sophisticated girl a slow, insolent smile, then followed Heath out into the warm, starbright night.

She'd never felt more reckless, more confident of herself. When she stole a secret glance at his profile, she had to smile. He was glum. She thought she understood that too; he didn't want her to leave Nicholson.

It was, as Beth had hinted, possible for her to get him to take her to dinner. Beyond that it was all up to her and she felt very confident – that night.

CHAPTER SEVEN

It was the following afternoon while Doctor Heath was examining a new admittee and was therefore absent from Ward B that her confidence got its worst jolt.

The painters had done a splendid job, the patients were lively in their vocal appreciation, but the smell of drying paint hadn't been dissipated when Doctor Fluornoy appeared in the doorway. He stopped dead still so no one actually saw him until he'd been standing there for perhaps a full sixty seconds. He'd wrinkled his nose first, then his iceberg eyes moved slowly up to the ceiling, down along the far wall, across to the doorways, and finally to the opened windows.

Ultimately, he turned to gaze stonily in the direction of the little office where Bonnie was going over some charts with Helen Cummings, her assistant. Neither of the girls had any idea Doctor Fluornoy was out there until a patient said with unnecessary vigour, 'Good afternoon Doctor Fluornoy.'

Bonnie heard the greeting, knew it was meant more as a warning to her than as a greeting for the chief surgeon, and felt her heart suddenly tighten as it skipped a beat. Miss Cummings fled from the office.

She kept right on with the desk-work, her back to the door, even when she heard old Fluornoy walking heavily around behind her and halt in the doorway. Her palms were damp. She tried very hard to assume the same light-hearted attitude she'd maintained the evening before with Albert Heath, but this was very different; this wasn't someone who was at least partially on her side.

'Miss Harper!'

She turned, smiled and arose. Fluornoy had his hands plunged deep into his pockets. His expression was the same as it'd been that first time they'd faced one another, out in the rose garden. Hostile.

'I was unaware any request had been made to redecorate Ward B.'

'No official request was made, Doctor Fluornoy,' she heard herself saying quietly.

'But it has been redecorated, has it not?'

'Yes, sir.'

'And I assume it was your doing.'

Fluornoy dropped his head slightly.

Because he was tall, gaunt and rawboned his appearance changed; he looked like some big bird of prey preparing to pounce.

'This was done on your own initiative, Miss Harper?'

'Yes sir. Do you – like it?'

'Can you give me one reason why I should like it?'

'It eliminated the sunglare, Doctor Fluornoy. It gives the ward a more warmly pleasant atmosphere. The effect on patient morale is–'

'Are you by any chance a psychologist, Miss Harper?'

'No sir. I'm simply someone who knows what it is like to feel as depressed and lonely and helpless as people feel in hospital wards.'

Outside, a cheery voice called out: 'Papers, folks.'

Bonnie winced. The paper boy might have come a half hour earlier or perhaps a half hour later. It would have been much better.

Doctor Fluornoy listened to the raised voices, the laughter and light banter as the paper boy went about the ward. His nostrils flared. He seemed to bristle without moving or changing his flinty expression. Then the iceberg eyes dropped to Bonnie again, lingered a moment and Doctor Fluornoy turned on his heel and stalked out of Ward B.

Bonnie heard someone call a flippant greeting to him, and flinched. Then she sank weakly down at the desk again, heart pounding. *Well,* she told herself mournfully, *you're sacked.*

She didn't see Doctor Heath the balance of that day although she searched for him and even asked the other nurses if he'd left word where he could be located. He hadn't, which in itself was very unusual.

She thought she knew what had happened; Doctor Fluornoy had encountered him somewhere and had, in his towering wrath, swept Albert along with him to Fluornoy's private office on the third floor. Poor Albert; he'd be getting skinned alive for what she'd done.

The balance of the day went very smoothly. Too smoothly in fact. None of the patients called for extra care which, if she'd been able to concentrate on that alone, would have encouraged her immensely. Helen Cummings came to her shortly before the dayshift departed to say in sepulchral tones she agreed absolutely with every innovation Bonnie had instituted.

That was a very weak pat on the back, though.

Later, at home and bathing, she wondered when the axe would fall. When the telephone rang at dinner she ran to get it, certain it would be some crisp voice from Nicholson, but it was one of Charles's clients. Later, when the three of them had an after-supper highball upon the verandah her brother-in-law asked what was troubling her. She told him.

Charles was unperturbed. He sipped his iced drink, hooked big feet over the verandah railing and said, 'Extraordinary,' in his deep, crisp voice. Beth was nearly as calm but not quite. She wanted to know whatever had possessed Bonnie to take such initiative. That brought forth the torrent of boiled-up resentment against Nicholson Hospital.

Charles finished his drink half way through the outburst, excused himself and went indoors. When he returned somewhat later he was smoking a cigar and looking as unruffled as ever. Into the silence between Beth and Bonnie he said, 'I cracked some ribs some years back in a yachting accident. I was at Nicholson for two days.' He exhaled grey smoke and turned to watch an auto coming uphill. 'As a matter of fact it *was* a depressing place. Put me in mind of a military hospital ward. Everyone excepting surgeons were addressed by their last names; no prefix, just Smith, Jones, Hamilton. Very efficient, as I recall, but very detached and impersonal.'

Bonnie looked round in surprise. Her brother-in-law was a staunch conservative. Her only previous encounter with him regarding the backwardness of his home-land had been deftly turned aside by Beth. Now, she sat gazing at his big frame, his placid, rugged features, and began to almost hope there might be a spark of adventure left in him.

'Of course they'll let you go,' he went on without looking at either Bonnie or his wife and from time to time glancing at the approaching auto as he relished his cigar. 'But I just called an acquaintance of mine who operates a private sanatorium in the suburbs. He has a place for you. In fact he said it was so hard getting qualified nurses he'd take it kindly if you'd come round for an interview first thing in the morning.'

Bonnie suddenly felt warm towards her brother-in-law, but before she could say anything, or even find the right words, Beth spoke up. 'Doctor Heath.'

The shiny auto had pulled in out at the kerbing.

Charles arose, gazed dubiously at the car a moment, blew out smoke and turned. 'Come along,' he said to his wife. 'I'm in need of another drink. You can accompany me.'

Beth went, but somewhat reluctantly. She was, after all, a woman, which meant she was interested in the possibilities she sensed; her sister was beautiful and Doctor Heath was handsome and unmarried. Charles herded her along into the house so by the time Albert Heath reached the porch only Bonnie was there to greet him. It wasn't a very enthusiastic greeting.

She said, 'Hullo.'

He didn't smile. 'Hullo.'

She made a feeble attempt to rally, saying, 'This would be better if it were a convention of undertakers. I'll be round for my cheque in the morning.' She added the last as a means of easing it for him; she thought she knew what he'd come to tell her. She'd been fired.

He didn't concede that point one way or the other. He instead took a chair uninvited, sat next to her and threw a long, slow look at the lights below out as far as the harbour. 'Another beautiful night,' he murmured, not looking at her. 'By the way, I had quite a discussion with Doctor Fluornoy.'

'You didn't have to defend me, Albert.'

This time he caught the name and turned, loosely smiling. 'I didn't, actually. In fact I didn't have an opportunity. I stood and listened. I'm very good at that. Learnt it as Administrator. Sit and listen or stand and listen. It's more tiresome standing, but it achieves the same result; the other person gets it all off his – or her – chest, runs out of breath, and I'm more or less unscathed.'

'Not this time I'll bet.'

He smiled a little more broadly. 'Well; old Fluornoy's had a bit of practice at skinning people.'

'I really didn't mean to get you into it, Albert.'

'Didn't you, love? Then you're hair-triggered. After all I'm supervising medic in Ward B, you know. He'd go after me first.'

She looked at the hands in her lap. That really hadn't occurred to her until old Fluornoy had gone stalking out of the little office. After a bit she said, 'What, specifically, did he say?'

He leaned back in the chair. 'It would

embarrass me to tell you. Did you know he'd been a military surgeon? Well he had; for quite a few years in fact. He can use profanity in the most interesting couplets I've ever heard.'

'That bad? I'm terribly sorry.'

Doctor Heath didn't hear, or chose to ignore, what she said. 'But what it all boiled down to was that he wanted you replaced as Ward Nurse.'

She flung up her head in astonishment. 'Just replaced?'

'Sampson's out of it of course. I told him I'd be perfectly agreeable, but which other Ward Nurse should we bring in? He ticked off a few names. I suggested he ask the women. He called two while I was in his office. They both threw it right back in his face. I thought he'd have a stroke. It seems that Ward B has suddenly become a very controversial area at Nicholson. No one wants to step into the mess at all. Well; I suggested he call the placement registry for a qualified woman. He did that too. There are no experienced Ward Nurses currently in the unemployed file.'

Watching his face, she saw the smile brighten. He was actually enjoying himself as he drawled out this recount of his encounter with John Fluornoy.

'He then said I'd have to take over.' For a moment there was nothing more said. 'I told him under no circumstances would I do that. He said he'd sack me. I told him he was too late – I'd just decided to quit.'

Bonnie gasped, her heart sinking. 'You didn't!'

He ignored that also. He was thoroughly enjoying himself. 'I felt sorry for him. He sat there looking helpless, red as a beet and slumped in his chair. I suggested that he talk with you. He said it wouldn't do a damned bit of good; that he'd seen enough of you; that you are one of those confounded activists who go about carrying placards and crying out against discrimination. I said I'd talk to you. He said that would be about as worthwhile as a starving person saying he wouldn't eat the first food he saw. Finally, he said *he'd* talk to you in the morning.'

'I won't go,' she exclaimed with spirit. 'I'm not going to let him humiliate me just to hand me my pay packet afterwards.'

'That's just it, duck. He's not going to sack you. He can't.'

She thought on that a moment. While she was doing this he swung his chair a bit to gaze at her and urged her to go ahead and see Doctor Fluornoy. His reason was sound.

'He tried to replace you. It didn't work. He almost lost a staff doctor – me. The registry has no one available and Nicholson is very short-handed as you know. Also, Ward B doesn't have a single vacant bed. The circumstances are definitely all in your favour. The worst he can do is–'

'Yes I know.'

'No you don't know. He won't sack you but he's going to make you smart. On the way up here I evolved what I believe may be the right approach for you.'

'Go on.'

'Don't be rude to him. Listen to everything he has to say. Adopt the same strategy I used as Administrator; let him get it all out; let him unwind and run down. Then quietly explain why you did it and–'

'He knows why I did it. I explained to him this afternoon.'

'Tell him again. But sweetly. Don't lose your temper whatever you do. Be conciliatory. Be appealing – you can do that just by standing in front of him. I know. You made my toughest resolve turn to water once. And when you've finished with all the justifications, promise you'll conform.'

She looked at his triumphant expression

and weakened. 'All right, Albert. But there's just one more thing – flowers in the ward?'

His smile collapsed. He groaned aloud and slumped in the chair rolling his eyes heavenward. She stood up, bent down and kissed him. He looked as astonished as she'd looked that night he'd kissed her.

'That,' she said, 'was for being my champion.'

CHAPTER EIGHT

She got two calls from Doctor Fluornoy's secretary and both times when she explained she just could not leave at the moment their meeting was postponed.

She hadn't been procrastinating either. There were two accident cases, an irate transferee from Ward A – a politician who could have got a private room but who sounded off like a foghorn to be moved into Ward B. There was also a Japanese seaman who'd been badly injured when a winch slipped on the ship-loading docks. Doctor Heath tended him at once with several of the squat, husky, stone-faced other Japanese seamen standing by. They had brought their friend in.

The man required prompt surgery. Albert sent Bonnie to call upstairs and alert Doctor Fluornoy. She helped put the seaman on the lift then returned to Ward B just as word was brought that Sampson wished to see her over in Ward A.

She didn't go; as she explained to the nurse who brought the message, she was just too rushed at the moment.

Half the day went like that. The second half wasn't quite as hectic but just when things slackened up a bit they returned with the Japanese seaman. He was as limp as an old rag and smelt powerfully of anaesthetic. She asked her nurses to go among the other patients asking for quiet.

Finally, near five o'clock, Albert returned looking tired. He'd assisted Fluornoy with the surgery on her Japanese sailor. She asked what the man's chances were. He gazed over at the puffy feverish face and shrugged. 'Fifty-fifty. He really should be put into a private room for two or three days.'

'He'll be all right here,' she told him, and left when a nurse beckoned. When she looked back Albert was heading out of the ward.

Finally, the ward grew quiet, the sun sank beyond some huge old trees outside and Bonnie used the tiny office to change into her street clothes. She didn't get out of the ward until a little after six. By that time the night crew was on duty. She went over the fresh charts with the Night Ward Sister giving specific instructions for the care of the Japanese, who would doubtless come round during the second shift.

The Night Nurse listened, nodded, and finally said, 'Bonnie; I want you to know I dragged my feet all the way in, tonight, because I was sure they'd have replaced you.'

Her answer to that was simple and accompanied with a perky little smile. 'They would have if they could've got anyone to take the job, and no doubt they still will as soon as they can. 'Night and good luck.'

The moment she stepped into her sister's house her brother-in-law met her. 'I thought you were going round to that sanatorium I told you about? That chap's been calling me all day long asking where you were?'

She gulped and stood big-eyed. She'd entirely forgot. 'Oh Charles, I'm so dreadfully sorry.'

'You forgot.'

'Yes. Please forgive me, will you?'

Charles slowly smiled. 'You look too much like a child caught with her hand in the cookie jar for me to be angry, but will you please call the man and tell him that you are, or are not, coming out, and get me off the hook with him?'

'Immediately,' she said, and fled to her room.

But the gentleman who operated the sanatorium was not easily put off. He asked what Bonnie got at Nicholson then added one-third more to it. She tried explaining that until she knew what would happen at Nicholson she wouldn't be available and he said, 'Miss Harper, believe me, there's no future at Nicholson. Aside from being an old tyrant Doctor Fluornoy runs that place as though it were a concentration camp. Half my staff and two-thirds of my patients have been at Nicholson. I have their stories to substantiate what I say. You have very limited opportunities there.'

She finally said that if she left Nicholson and decided to remain in the nursing field, she'd come to see him, then rang off just as Beth called her for dinner. She didn't have a chance to bathe first as was her custom, nor even to change her dress.

Charles asked what the latest developments were. She had to admit the day had been simply hectic in the routine way. But she told them she was to see Doctor Fluornoy the next day. Neither her sister nor brother-in-law persisted in that topic. Beth told of her day at home and Charles told several amusing anecdotes, then the subjects to be discussed drifted back and forth. It was a pleasant meal and relaxed Bonnie completely. Afterwards, while Beth and Charles went to the verandah for a highball and to watch the day die, Bonnie went after that bath and change she needed.

She felt so much better. The bath completed for her what the jolly dinner had begun. Whether her sister and Charles had deliberately made an effort to help her unwind, or not, they'd most certainly succeeded.

She lay in the bath thinking of people; of Beth and Charles of course, because they'd prompted the thought, but also of the nurses at Nicholson, of Elvira Sampson of John Fluornoy, of Bryan, and of Albert Heath.

She had an unusual thought concerning Doctor Fluornoy; the basis for it was that while he'd opposed her, he'd done it always as a man satisfied within the narrow confines of procedures he'd followed so long he knew no other procedures. He'd never actually opposed her as a man whose private ideas clashed with her own ideas.

It was a nebulous train of thought yet she lay there pursuing it, and by the time she left the bath and stepped into her adjoining bedroom to re-dress, she'd developed both an idea and a theory. The idea she'd test when she had to face Doctor Fluornoy tomorrow, the theory she'd keep a secret until she'd satisfied herself it could be correct.

Beth rapped on the door. 'Bonnie; Doctor Heath is here. We're having a highball on the verandah. Hurry along when you can.'

She didn't hurry at all. Just to be arbitrary she changed her dress again, put on something light blue, the colour of sea-water. She brushed her hair an extra lick too. Then she laughed at herself: she wasn't doing any of this to make Albert Heath wait, she was doing it because she wanted his eyes to pop wide open when she appeared.

They did. He arose, glass in hand, when she stepped on to the porch, his expression showing definite and undisguised admiration. Charles also rose, but looked at her as a barrister might consider some lovely witness who'd been told how to dress in order to melt a jury's collective heart. He said he'd fetch her a drink and disappeared inside.

Beth broke the interlude of staring with a gentle remark about the evening. 'I love this time of year. The days may get hot after a bit, but usually there's the sea breeze, isn't there? And the nights are heavenly.'

Albert nodded, watched Bonnie come forward to a chair and said, 'Quite.' He would have held Bonnie's chair but it would have been too obvious; he'd have had to move around Beth.

Bonnie said something about the man from the sanatorium. Albert's head shot up. His eyes looked stricken up until she explained how she'd got clear, then he relaxed and sipped his drink, eventually saying, 'Remember what I told you, Bonnie; anyone can quit. It takes something more to carry on.'

Charles returned with Bonnie's highball, and two cigars. Albert declined the smoke. He didn't use tobacco. Not, he hastily explained, because he felt it was especially detrimental to health despite all the hulla-baloo about that, but simply because as a youth he'd got sick on the stuff he'd never had the courage to try again.

It was pleasant, sitting relaxed and friendly. They were a compatible group. It would of course have been impossible for Beth and Charles not to have felt electricity about them in the moonlit shadows, but until they decided they'd done their duty as hosts neither made any move to return to the house.

Charles and Albert discussed Dominion politics. Since neither had any radical viewpoints it was a watered-down, comfortable discussion. Albert brought Bonnie and Beth into the conversation when he could, which was something Charles seldom did, not that he objected especially, but Charles was something of a Turk where women were concerned.

It wasn't a very noticeable thing except within the family. He treated Beth wonderfully; whatever she wanted she got. But Charles's word was law. Fortunately Beth's disposition was such that she accepted this completely. Where other women would have rebelled violently, Beth was far too wise for that, hence she and her husband made an ideal pair.

Albert turned from time to time to look

past Beth to Bonnie. Moonlight played tricks. No one knew that better than women. She could feel his eyes on her. She understood more than he'd have thought, too. Female intuition was a quite powerful but little-known factor in the masculine world.

When Charles and Beth finally left and went inside, Bonnie could feel the atmosphere quicken, could feel the night get warmer and the starshine turn whiter. She said, 'Did you look in on the Japanese sailor before you left tonight?'

'Yes. The man's got a rugged body. I'm sure he'll make it all right. His friends came round shortly before I left bringing some incense. They said it would ease his anxieties. Of course I had the stuff put in your office. It might ease *his* anxieties but we can't have forty-nine other patients awakening in the morning thinking they've been spirited to some Far Eastern temple, can we?'

She didn't answer. She liked the idea of scented incense and dwelt on it until he mentioned Sampson. That brought her mind back to the present with a small jolt. She'd really meant to look in on Sampson.

'She was a little perturbed,' he said. 'I

stopped by for a moment before going home.'

Bonnie smiled at him. 'Miss Sampson's never a *little* perturbed, Albert. She's never a *little* anything.'

He laughed softly nodding his head. 'You're right. Anyway she's coming along quite well. I think it's her indignation that's partly responsible.'

'Painted walls?' said Bonnie. 'Newspapers?'

'And slack discipline among your nurses.'

Bonnie sighed. 'Do Tartars ever change, Albert?'

He didn't know but he doubted it. Then he brought up something she hadn't thought much about. 'When she comes back to Ward B it's going to go hard on your nurses.'

After a moment of reflection Bonnie said, 'And my patients.'

'Well yes, although they change constantly. I was thinking on the drive up here: would Doctor Fluornoy assign her to another ward and leave you in charge in Ward B?'

'It's hard to imagine,' she murmured, and got back to thinking about her private assessment of John Fluornoy. 'I imagine he'd be doubtful of having me in charge of anything.'

'I wouldn't, Bonnie.'

She looked at his soft profile in the shadows. 'You're different though. You're very sweet.'

He had started to say something else but after that he was momentarily silent. Eventually, putting aside the empty highball glass he said, 'Would you care to take a drive up along the coast? It's still early and the night is too beautiful to be wasted.'

She arose. 'I'll get a sweater.'

She felt his eyes on her as she turned houseward.

Inside, Charles and Beth were reading. Beth looked up but Charles only absently smiled as she marched past. But, when she'd gone, his grave glance sought his wife's face. He gave her a droll wink.

In the bedroom Bonnie stood a moment before her mirror. Every girl knows somehow when that special moment has arrived. She may have gone on a dozen dates with a man, all more or less the same, but when that one special moment arrives she knows it.

Bonnie stood before the mirror. She was not particularly fond of jewellery, never had been, but she was young and very lovely; she needed no highlights to enhance her eyes or hair, her smile or figure.

She brushed her hair to heighten the shine, and touched her lips to add a mite more colour, but otherwise she simply got the cardigan from a closet and was ready.

Nicholson, Doctor Fluornoy, the crises she'd caused, all dropped away. Only one thing mattered this night. She already knew how *she* felt; had known for several weeks so there was no need for recapitulation, for doubt, for timidity. What she would shortly discover was how *he* felt, and she thought she had that answer too. But he had to tell her.

She returned to the parlour, told Beth she was going driving with Doctor Heath, and walked outside. Again, Charles and Beth exchanged a significant look, and a little smile.

CHAPTER NINE

There was a fair amount of traffic until they reached the seashore, then, where ordinarily on such a balmy night they'd have encountered quite heavy traffic, they had the up-country carriageway almost to themselves. At least there was no congestion and the farther they drove the fewer headlights they encountered.

He pointed out several landmarks and when she asked how long he'd been in the islands he said four years; since leaving medical school for his internship. She considered that and said something about him having served an unusually long internship. He smiled.

'You know Doctor Fluornoy. He believes in 'em. I would imagine as a young man he believed in long engagements too, but I don't.'

She didn't press that oblique subject he'd introduced. She said, adhering to her original idea, 'You certainly seem to know the countryside.'

'My relaxation,' he said, patting his steering wheel.

She had an unkind thought: she recalled the redhead and imagined she'd be a very willing passenger on auto rides. All she said, though, was, 'Are you planning on staying here?'

'Odd you should ask. I've been wondering about that since stepping up to my present status. I could go back to England, of course. There's always the shortage there.

Or perhaps to America. Possibly Canada.'
He looked at her. 'What would you advise?'

She wouldn't. 'There is only one person who can advise you, Albert. You.'

'But you've been to some of those places.'

She pointed to the mechanically revolving beam far out and asked its name. He said New Zealand's underwater reefs and bouldered shores had, in the early sailing days, accounted for a goodly number of the wrecked ships in the Pacific. He named that light and named several more which were strung up and down the coast. Finally, slowing a bit, he said, 'You avoided my question.'

She hadn't avoided it, she said, so much as she'd declined to answer it. 'What I would see of a hospital and what you'd see are quite different you know. I'm only a nurse. You're a physician. Anyway, after four years at Nicholson I suppose most hospitals would seem somewhat the same. It would be a matter of adjusting to new routines is about all, I should judge. Although there'd most certainly be other very noticeable differences.'

The last sentence brought a mildly pained expression to his face but he said nothing. They drove to where a light dip existed, turned off on to a short, rutted little road facing the ocean, and halted beneath two huge old straggly trees. He twisted on the seat.

'Care to walk along the beach, or would it fill your shoes with sand?'

She hid a smile. That redhead must have been quite a problem, not liking sand in her shoes and all. 'I'll go barefoot,' she said, turned, alighted, kicked off her shoes, removed both stockings while he was still on the opposite side of the car, then straightened up to see that he'd tossed his sweater back upon the seat.

It seemed even warmer next to the sea, for some reason. They walked to the end of their little road, stepped off into the sand, and paced slowly along. He felt for her fingers. She didn't resist not withdraw her hand, but that personal touch did something to her; she couldn't have ignored it if she'd wanted to – which she didn't.

'That's a beautiful home your sister and brother-in-law have,' he said, turning northward at the water's edge. 'Everyone has an idea that someday they'd like to have one just like it.'

'Would you?'

'Yes. But not alone; and if I had my choice I'd like to have it somewhat closer to those hills above Nicholson.'

She sighed.

He looked round quickly. 'What was that for?'

'Nothing particular,' she murmured and tugged him along.

'You don't like Nicholson,' he mumbled, responding to her pull.

'Albert; it's not that I don't *like* Nicholson, it's simply that Nicholson is so old-fashioned. I don't dare say that to my brother-in-law who is very proud of having been born here, or to Doctor Fluornoy, but I'll tell *you:* Nicholson's procedures are twenty-five years behind the times.'

He stopped and, holding her hand, caused her to also stop. 'All right, Bonnie,' he exclaimed earnestly. 'I've never denied that. But you've made a start at changing things. That ought to make you *like* Nicholson.'

'You're being naïve,' she retorted. 'Albert, you know perfectly well I'll be sacked the moment Sampson can come back, or as soon as Doctor Fluornoy can find another experienced Ward Nurse.'

He slowly shook his head. 'I've been doing some thinking about that. I doubt that you'll get it, Bonnie.'

She stood in the cool sand looking up at

him. If he had a doubt it would be a rational one. She had no doubt at all, so her curiosity was piqued. 'Why not?'

'For one thing by the time you could be replaced John Fluornoy will see that you've actually heightened morale not only among patients but among nurses and visitors as well, at least one hundred per cent. And for another thing, when I told him I'd quit last week, he didn't like that at all. So if he sacks you I resign on the spot. Then there is something else, love. I'm not precisely sure old Fluornoy isn't on your side.'

That interested her; it also happened to fit the private notion concerning old Doctor Fluornoy she had. 'He hasn't acted like it, Albert. In fact he's acted just the opposite.'

He reached, caught her other hand and smiled a little, softly and tenderly. 'Not even young rebels can adopt a rapid and revolutionary change in one glance, Bonnie. Those things take time.'

'I'm not sure I have any time left, Albert, or at least not very *much* time left.'

He raised her arms and gently pulled. 'That's my part of it. I'll see to it that you *get* the time.'

She didn't resist his pull. When they were close enough he dropped her hands to hold her by the upper arms and lower his head. She'd have had plenty of time to twist free, had she wanted to.

The kiss was soft and almost painfully pleasant. When he straightened back he was still gently smiling at her. He said nothing. Neither did she. They simply turned and began walking again.

The night around them was a blending of sea-scent and cooling land. They saw a bonfire far ahead down the beach closer to the city and also saw a great tailrace of light where a meteor scratched its searing imprint across the underbelly of heaven. Back where trees stood beyond the sand, planted there in decades gone to hold back the inevitable erosion caused by high tides, the moon rode aloofly upon its ordained course.

He suddenly said, speaking slowly which seemed to be his manner when he was being careful what he said, 'Bonnie; have you thought of marrying; of settling down in one place for the balance of your life?'

It sounded so solemn she shot him a sidewards look. It made him seem much older than he was. 'I've thought of it, Albert. Every girl does, sometime, after she stops being a child.'

'Well...'

'Yes?'

'Well ... perhaps we'd better turn around. We've come quite a distance from the car.'

They turned. She didn't look at him for a long while expecting him to take up the topic where he'd lamely dropped it but he never did. They walked for almost a half hour in silence then some people up ahead hooting back and forth as they ran towards the surf distracted him. He watched, slowing his pace a little.

She slowed to also watch. The swimmers were young and noisily exuberant. The first one to hit the water let out a great wail saying it was cold. The others laughingly splashed in and also cried out.

Albert picked up the gait again. They walked on past with their shadows on the starboard side, sometimes in water, sometimes elongated on the sand.

They were only a short distance from the auto before he stopped again, turned her and faced the sea. 'Do you like boats?' he asked. She nodded. She liked boats fine; she also liked men who finished what they started. 'Would you like to go out with me someday? I do a little off-shore fishing. It's great recreation.'

She was sure that it was splendid

recreation and said without any great enthusiasm that she'd like to go fishing with him, sometime. She also said she'd been thinking about that position at the private sanatorium and that perhaps it might be wise of her to accept the position out there before it was filled, and before she was sacked at Nicholson.

That brought him around facing her. 'I thought we'd settled that,' he said, his expression grave. 'You were going to give Nicholson a chance.'

She shrugged. She'd thought it had been settled too, but at the moment she was feeling perverse. 'I won't do anything drastic like quitting tomorrow, but don't you think a person alone should look out for themselves first?'

He didn't argue the point, but he said, 'Bonnie, I'm trying to help, so you're hardly alone.'

She looked down where that bonfire was little more than a pinprick of orange light. 'I don't want to get you into trouble, Albert. I don't want you to have to quit or get on the bad side of Doctor Fluornoy.' She lifted her face to him. Moonlight fell across her making soft shadows and soft highlights. 'We'd better be getting back, hadn't we?'

He didn't move.

She could feel the atmosphere changing between them. It was almost as though something physical was there with them. He said very softly, 'Bonnie, I love you. I'm not sure how that happened. I'm past thirty and it's never been like this at all before. I think – it was that day you came into the office and got mad at me.'

She stood perfectly still scarcely breathing. She might have helped him along but she didn't. She knew what the singing in her own heart meant. She also knew if he opened his arms she'd run into them.

'I – uh – have been leading up to this all evening – only that damned hospital or old Fluornoy, or something else kept interfering.' He looked almost desperate, standing stiffly and very earnestly before her. 'Also, I had no idea this would be so difficult to say – to explain.'

She finally *did* help him. 'Don't stop now, Albert.'

He looked very gradually relieved. 'Well; I didn't know how you'd take it.'

'I'm still here, Albert. I haven't run to the car.'

'Yes. Well; what I brought you down here to say was... Now you don't have to answer this right away, you understand.'

She understood. She understood perfectly and it was agonizing standing there two feet apart waiting for him to get it all said so she could pour out her own feelings.

Then he faltered again. 'Bonnie I'd better just take you home. I'm sorry if I've put you in an awkward position. If I've taken advantage of the fact that we're alone down here, and all that.'

He reached, took her elbow, turned and started walking. Just for a moment she almost rebelled; almost planted her feet flat-down in the sand and wrenched round to make him face her again. But she didn't. She did cast a sidelong look at his very serious face. He looked almost grim. She sighed and paced along.

He discreetly moved to the opposite side of the car while she put her stockings and shoes back on, then they climbed in and he started the engine. There was one more moment, right there, when he sat behind the wheel with both hands upon it wrestling with some thought, but when she was daring to hope again, he meshed gears, backed around and headed back towards the multi-lighted city.

When they pulled up out front of the

house he helped her out. By then he was himself again. He held her hand for a moment before they parted then pulled her close, kissed her in that same gentle manner, and she ran for the house.

In the privacy of her own room she sat on the side of the bed for a moment waiting for the disturbance in her heart to subside. He'd come so *awfully* close; so wonderfully close to asking her to marry him. She looked at herself in the mirror.

Then she put both hands over her face and laughed.

He was a sophisticated, highly educated mature man. Remembering the svelte redhead she also surmised he was an experienced person. Yet when he'd come face to face with something as serious as marriage and his wish for it, he'd crumpled like a schoolboy.

She laughed at him and inwardly cried for him at the same time. She could even imagine that right now he was pacing the floor of his apartment in the city troubled and perhaps even angry with himself.

She was perfectly correct. That's exactly what he was doing. The only thing she didn't know was that he had a highball glass in his hand as he paced.

CHAPTER TEN

The following morning as soon as she had a free moment she crossed the hall to Ward A and hunted up Elvira Sampson. She didn't expect a pleasant visit and she wasn't wrong. Miss Sampson saw her approaching long before she got near the bed. Sampson was ready and waiting.

'Well, Harper,' the growling voice snapped. 'You've certainly upset everything haven't you? I knew – I knew as well as I knew my own name that if they let you take over, something like this would happen!'

Bonnie stood waiting, but after a bit it almost seemed as though Sampson wouldn't run out of denunciations or breath either. She raked Bonnie over the coals for having the ward redecorated. She mentioned the newspapers sarcastically. She made several slurring allusions to other changes. When she finally did run out of accusations – and breath – she said, 'I suppose you'll be wanting carpeting on the floor next.'

Bonnie reached automatically to smooth the pillow and adjust the turned-down sheet. 'I hope you can come back soon, Miss Sampson,' she softly said, making no defence against, nor even alluding to, any of the things Sampson had upbraided her about. 'And I'm sorry I couldn't get over here sooner. I tried yesterday but it was a rush from morning until evening.'

Sampson's tough old eyes studied Bonnie's composed face. 'They'll fire you, of course, Harper. You realize that don't you?'

Bonnie smiled gently. 'I realize it. Is there anything I can bring you?'

'Nothing. I only wanted to let you know I don't approve of any of your insane innovations either. That's all!'

On the way back to Ward B Bonnie ran into the lanky newcomer who'd taken over Albert Heath's former job, Doctor Bryan. She knew his type; had pegged him that first day they'd met while Albert had still been in the administration section. He would have stopped to smile and talk but she briskly nodded, cut him off without faltering her stride, and swept straight on through into Ward B.

She went along to look at the Japanese

sailor. He was conscious. According to his chart he'd come round early the previous night. The man looked bewildered, small and apprehensive. Bonnie brought forth a glass ashtray from one pocket, a little conical piece of the incense his friends had brought him from another pocket, lit the incense, set it upon his bedstand in the ashtray and watched his black gaze show surprise. When she smiled he smiled back.

'Your friends brought it,' she said, referring to the incense.

The sailor said he was very grateful. He also asked what his condition was. She didn't know; she'd have to study his chart then talk to the doctor, but she promised to do both and return when she could. The Japanese didn't take his eyes off her until she'd gone down near the lower end of the ward to talk to another patient. Then he breathed deeply of his incense and shortly afterwards fell asleep.

She met Albert shortly before meal time at midday. He said the sailor was progressing well. 'Exceptionally well in fact. I knew he was rugged and healthy. I just didn't know *how* rugged. I should imagine, without difficulties, he might be up and about within ten days.'

She asked about several other patients, particularly about the loud-mouthed politician who was suffering from high blood pressure and looked it, being restless, demanding and florid. Albert nodded a little, understanding the basis for her concern.

'There always have to be a few of that type,' he consoled.

She had an answer for him. 'At least, when he knows what he wants, he has no difficulty finding the words to ask for it.'

Albert, flipping through charts, lifted his eyes and quizzically gazed at her. She was chagrined with herself the moment she'd made the innuendo and swiftly spoke of other things.

'I'll be going up to see Doctor Fluornoy in a few minutes; have to do while there's time in here. Also, I burnt some of that incense for the sailor.'

He soberly nodded. He had smelled it upon entering the ward. 'Thought for a moment I was in a josh house,' he murmured.

She left him in the office when one of her girls came. The politician, whose name was Fred McCann, was making loud, unpleasant remarks about the incense.

She went up to McCann's bed wearing her sweet smile. He let go a verbal blast and without losing her smile she said quietly, 'If you don't like it I'll have you moved back to Ward A, Mister McCann. That sailor had surgery yesterday; he's very ill. Your loudness isn't good for him or for anyone else in here. In Ward B we make it a point to appreciate each other's problems, and to help. You can do that, or you can leave. It's up to you.'

Fred McCann's florid, heavy face looked disbelieving. Bonnie, already looking so young and girlish, still was smiling. He had just been read off in a musical voice by a very beautiful girl who had smiled all through it and who was still smiling. There was no anger, no fear of him, no trembling. He opened and closed his mouth. He rolled his head to the left. A dark, wizened older man was watching him with candid hostility. He rolled his head to the right. A much younger and larger man was gazing stonily at him from that side.

Bonnie bent to adjust the sheet and fluff up his pillow. She was almost laughing at him now, her eyes as merry as though they'd just shared a joke. They had, but it was on him.

He said, 'Righto, Miss Harper. No harm intended. By the way; when I was in Ward A a Miss Sampson over there told me some wild tales about what you were doing over here. As a member of the local treasury-disbursement committee, I had to come see for myself.' McCann winked. 'Barring the incense I think you've done a smash-up job in here. I'm not sure I even want to return home.'

They parted friends.

Doctor Fluornoy's secretary called just as Bonnie returned to the little ward-office. She said she'd be right up, rang off and went in search of her daytime assistant – Helen Cummings – to say where she'd be. Albert and Miss Cummings were going over the therapy schedule up at the far end of the ward. The moment Bonnie said where she was going Albert handed the treatment schedule to Miss Cummings and accompanied Bonnie out into the glistening corridor.

He acted both glum and hopeful. 'Remember now, don't lose your temper. Be as sweet as you usually are.'

She nodded, having already had that advice from him previously and having already decided to follow it.

He squeezed her hand. 'Good luck, love.'

She walked away and when Doctor Heath heard someone mention his name he turned and went back into Ward B looking harassed and just a trifle rebellious, which was not a normal reaction for him, to anything at all.

Doctor Fluornoy's secretary was a very polished middle-aged woman with beautiful grey hair, an alabaster complexion and a sturdy physique. She was poised, calm and in command. Doctor Fluornoy was being detained in consultation, she informed Bonnie, bringing up a chair for the younger woman, but he'd be along in a moment or two.

Bonnie sat, glanced surreptitiously at her wristwatch, and murmured something pleasant about the weather. The older woman wisely smiled. Her light blue eyes were kindly.

'He's really not such a terrible man, Miss Harper,' she soothingly said. 'Of course, you are something a little special. He told me of meeting you the day you interrupted him in the rose garden.'

The blue eyes brightened with silent amusement.

Bonnie responded; she liked this older woman with the perfect poise. She didn't know her although they'd spoken several times on the telephone, and she'd also seen the secretary in the cafeteria a number of times.

'You *have* given him a few bad moments, Miss Harper,' the deep, calm voice went on. 'In fact I had all I could manage keeping from doubling over with laughter the day he stormed in here to tell me you'd had Ward B redecorated without consulting anyone.'

Bonnie's lips drooped. 'It didn't make me want to laugh,' she said, in recollection. 'I thought he was going to take a switch to me.'

'Miss Harper; you don't know him. It takes a long while. I've been his secretary for eleven years.'

'But he was furious all the same.'

The light eyes kindled again. 'He was most certainly upset, but not really furious. You see, he's cultivated a crustiness, but primarily that is because he cannot abide anything being slipshod. I don't mean your ward. I mean laxness. He's a great believer in discipline; in hewing to the line. But very often he wears that hostile expression just to keep people from taking up his time. Or because he wants them to quake a little.'

Bonnie weakly smiled. 'A little? I was still

quaking when I got home that night.'

'You're not quaking now are you?'

'Not yet but I will be the minute he walks through that door.'

As though on cue the long, gaunt form of John Fluornoy appeared out of the corridor. He was wearing an unbuttoned white ward-jacket and had both hands thrust into the pockets, which pulled the garment out of shape. He looked more than ever like a rawboned old bird of prey about to pounce.

He looked down at Bonnie. She arose at once. He didn't say a word but stepped into the room, removed the white coat and looked at it. 'Miss Singleton,' he growled at his secretary without looking at her, 'have this confounded thing fumigated, please. I've just come from Ward B. They're burning *incense* in there now!'

He turned back, looked straight at Bonnie, stepped past into his private office and said, 'Miss Harper; please step in here.'

Bonnie and the secretary exchanged a look. Miss Singleton gave her head a little negative wag and winked. Bonnie wasn't sure that meant she wasn't to be afraid, or that she was to be.

She entered the office, pushed up a smile and waited until Doctor Fluornoy closed the door and stepped behind his desk. He asked her to be seated. Since there were only two chairs and he was occupying one, she took the other one. It was directly in front of his littered desk. She'd have felt better standing but it wasn't anything to make an issue about.

He let off a big sigh, leaned back, swung and gazed out the small window in the north wall of his office. There was a brilliant splash of sunshine outside. He said, 'Miss Harper... That incense perhaps has some psychological value for the Japanese gentleman, but didn't it strike you as about as foreign to a hospital ward as anything could be?'

She waited a moment, expecting him to swivel round and glare but he continued to sit slumped, gazing out the window. She framed her answer very carefully and said it.

'All my other patients are well on the way to becoming either ambulatory or discharged, Doctor Fluornoy. The Japanese sailor was among total strangers, not even of his own race. He was very ill and depressed. Only one patient said anything about the incense. A Mister McCann. The others were very considerate.'

He swung back. 'McCann, Miss Harper,

happens to be an influential person.'

'So he told me, Doctor Fluornoy.'

He grimaced. 'Yes, I imagine he did at that. Nonetheless, leaving McCann out of it – I want you to tell me where it'll stop?'

'Stop, sir…?'

'Yes, Miss Harper, where it will stop. The redecorating, the daily tour of that newsboy selling his blasted papers, the incense – where will it stop?'

She smiled at him, remembering what Albert had said. 'Doctor; isn't it almost as important to keep their minds occupied; to keep their spirits up?'

'Yes, of course it is, young lady. But do you realize there's talk all over the hospital, among patients, staff, visitors, about unorthodox Ward B?'

'No sir.'

'Did you know some newsmen called yesterday asking if they could come and interview me about our new policy at Nicholson?'

'No sir.' She had to struggle to keep that smile now.

'Well, they did, and I told them we had no new policy. That this was a hospital not a dancehall.' Fluornoy leaned forward across his desk. 'I realize Doctor Heath believes in

118

what you're doing. And I don't want you to get the idea I'm altogether against you. But I want one thing from you here and now – your word you'll make no new innovations without consulting me.'

She remembered what his secretary had said outside. She also felt a little glow of secret satisfaction that her own assessment hadn't been incorrect. She arose and now her smile was bright and warm.

'I promise,' she said.

CHAPTER ELEVEN

That evening Beth and Charles had a dinner to go to so when Albert Heath drove up Bonnie was alone on the verandah. She was also in good spirits. She'd scarcely made him welcome and he'd scarcely pulled a chair over closer, when she related her experience with Doctor Fluornoy.

He was pleased. 'I knew you could charm him.'

'I didn't charm him. I was frightened half to death. But his secretary told me a bit about him before he walked in, and moreover, since having been with him several times I've made an appraisal of my own. It's not that he's entirely against change at Nicholson, Albert, it's simply that he isn't certain what reactions might ensue.'

Albert sat a moment gazing out over the city then he soberly said, 'Yes. Well, there was a reaction you know.'

She swung. 'No I didn't know.'

'Yes. The hospital governing board came round this evening shortly before I left. They went through Ward B like a group of undertakers, then marched up to Fluornoy's office. They were still in there when I left over an hour later. I hung about hoping they'd come out and I could possibly hear something. It didn't work out that way.'

She looked at him and he returned her gaze. He nodded his head slightly as though to confirm her worst suspicions. She asked if he knew any of the board members. He didn't know any personally, but he'd heard plenty about them. They were local businessmen; successful businessmen in fact, and they were all about Doctor Fluornoy's age. 'And philosophy,' he said glumly. 'I suppose in the morning we'll hear what was said.'

This spoilt her evening. She faced forward

again. 'Just,' she murmured into the night, 'when it was beginning to look as though Nicholson might get out of the Stone Age.'

He grunted. The sound was non-committal. He raised both arms over his head in a mighty stretch, then slumped again. 'Beautiful night,' he muttered. 'I don't suppose you'd care to drive back down to the beach and walk in the sand?'

She wouldn't but she didn't say so. She instead arose to ask if he'd like a highball. He caught her wrist as she moved closer to his chair and looked up into her face.

'I'm not much of a drinker, really. Just never cultivated the habit.' He continued to hold her wrist and gaze upwards. She felt dampness on his hand and saw the way he seemed to brace after taking in a big breath. Then he dropped her arm.

'Bonnie; will you marry me?'

This time she'd had no warning. They weren't even close to the subject. She stood looking down at him. There were several confused moments when she said nothing and tried to get the unpleasant premonitions untangled from her personal feelings.

He stood up. 'It was poor timing, wasn't it? Well; at least now you know what I never quite got out last night so you can think about it.' He looked away and back again, made a crooked little self-conscious smile and said, 'I don't care what happens at Nicholson. The world's full of hospitals. Maybe there's one somewhere that *needs* creativity; that needs someone with life and imagination.'

She finally got the sorting out done, but she didn't feel quite the same tonight as she'd felt along the seashore the night before. Still; he'd asked it and she would answer.

'Of course I'll marry you, Albert.'

He had his lips parted to say something. He closed them. He squinted at her. He started to raise a hand as though to run it through his crisp blond hair, but checked that impulse to say. 'Well; that's fine.'

She leaned inward and raised upwards. His face came down to meet her. This time the kiss was a little more fiery, but she caught herself before the chemistry got them both embarrassed. She took him by the hand and turned to go down into the garden off the porch. He was perfectly willing.

There were no other homes close by and the yard had been terraced to give the best view. It also was well tended and had beautiful roses on each terrace. This was Charles's delight and hobby, this garden, and if he seemed at times staid, ultra-conservative, here in a natural element, he was daring and imaginative.

She led him to a hardy wooden bench where, with the house at their back and the city spread out below, they sat and felt, as well as saw, all the night-charm.

'If it could be different,' she said, not making too much sense right away with her words, 'it would be so much better. Albert; if I'd had any idea... I'd just have been a meek little mouse at Nicholson.' She turned impulsively. 'Why didn't I have some warning?'

He was a little baffled. She seemed to be speaking of two things simultaneously. He took her hand and held it. 'Forget Nicholson,' he said. 'At least for now, for tonight. There is just the two of us out here. Nicholson belongs to another world a million seconds away.'

She liked the way he'd said that. 'All right. But it'll still come down to Nicholson no matter what we say.'

'No it won't because we're not going to plan anything. Not tonight.'

He put an arm around her waist. She

leaned a little, twisting her face to meet his lips. She whispered, 'I love you, Albert; I've loved you for a long while.'

After the kiss he said, 'Even that day in the administration office when you got mad and cried?'

'That day particularly. I seldom cry. But that day you were the last person on earth I wanted to scold me.'

He lay her head upon his shoulder and kept the arm around her. She was still for a moment then said, 'See? Nicholson again.'

He smiled. 'Well; let it come, it's not going to ruin anything for either of us, I'll promise you that.'

A wide-swinging pair of auto lamps swung inward from the lower roadway as a car came carefully up the incline. He asked if that might be her sister and brother-in-law coming home. She didn't think so; the last thing Beth had confided to her was that those barrister dinners were the most long-winded, boring social events she knew of.

She straightened off his shoulder to watch the car. It wasn't making its approach the way anyone would drive who knew the road. 'A stranger,' she said. He turned in the opposite direction but there were no homes beyond the Hamilton residence. There were a few lower down, though, so he mentioned the possibility that the auto was going to stop at one of them. They stopped watching it for a bit.

He fished something from a pocket and fumbled with it in the weak moonlight, his head down, face averted, as he said, 'I felt like a sneak bringing this along, Bonnie. I wasn't sure I'd ever show it to you. See if it fits.'

The little box finally opened. She saw moonlight catch with a bluish flame in the solitary diamond of the engagement ring. For a moment she just sat and looked. Her heart was pounding. This was the moment every girl hoped – and knew – would someday arrive.

He took the ring in one hand, her finger in the other hand, and tried the ring on. It fitted perfectly, neither too loose nor too tight. He looked up, amazed. She had a wetness to her tremulous smile. She threw both arms round his neck, forgot everything except the ecstasy and the agony, and kissed him vehemently.

They clung together without speaking. A dog barked down the hill a short distance and behind them in a great gaunt old tree a nightbird of some kind made a disgruntled sound as though the barking dog had awakened him. They scarcely heard at all.

When she dared, she pulled back and said, 'You have no idea how long I've been waiting for you, Albert.'

He was just a trifle pragmatic about that. 'At twenty, love, it can't have been too long.'

'Oh but it *has* been. A girl starts dreaming when she's quite young. The dream gets stronger as time passes, but it starts out a lot sooner than a man would think.' She looked upwards. 'And you?'

He was honest. 'Well; of course the first time I saw you, I certainly noticed you. In fact I thought about you off and on all the remainder of that day. But *love* – I knew that last week. Then I rehearsed exactly how I'd tell you. But it's really rather difficult, you know. It's one thing to speak of love among friends, even among female friends, but when one really feels love, it's just not easy to describe nor even say.'

'Like last night?'

He nodded ruefully. 'I made a frightful mess of that didn't I?'

She didn't answer but she gave a start and so did he as someone up the terrace several yards loudly cleared a masculine throat. They sprang up.

Doctor Fluornoy said gravely, 'Good evening. I'm awfully sorry to be intruding. I'd have gone back except that after coming up that confounded road round there I need to catch my breath. Do you mind?'

They simply stared. Doctor John Fluornoy in the Hamilton garden was about as expected as Mephistopheles would have been. He squinted at the stair-stepped little path and came down a little closer to them.

'This is a very lovely spot,' he said without much enthusiasm because he was concentrating on the little path. 'Not exactly my cup of tea, as it were, clambering up and down mountainsides, but really quite lovely.'

He stopped, sighed, looked past at the star-lighted city below, then looked at them. He wasn't smiling but Bonnie got the distinct impression he was very close to it; either that, or laughter. He looked at Albert longest.

'Good to see you have some outside activities, Doctor. I've always maintained for a medical practitioner, the best way to maintain physical tone and mental alertness is healthy outdoor activities.'

Bonnie laughed first. Albert finally also laughed, but it was a trifle hollow. Doctor

Fluornoy was grinning from ear to ear. Evidently surprising them under those amorous circumstances had first shocked, then delighted, him.

'And you,' the older man said to Bonnie. 'Not enough turning hospital into a three-ring circus. You have to win away my most promising staff member. Young lady, you simply have too much energy for any one body.'

She said if he'd like to go back to the verandah she'd bring out some tea, or perhaps a highball if he'd prefer. Fluornoy clasped both hands behind his back and said, 'No thank you, Miss Harper. I had supper only a short while ago.' Then he stood as he often did, looking at them with a bit of a bleak face, and let the moments tick off until he was ready to speak again.

'There was a meeting of the hospital governing board, this evening. The gentlemen went through Ward B. It seems they'd been contacted by some newsmen about new policies at Nicholson.'

Fluornoy paused. Albert shot Bonnie a look and she shot one straight back. They both already knew as much as he'd said. There was more and they braced for that.

'The gentlemen were surprised, Miss

Harper, that a nurse would take it upon herself to redecorate her ward. They were even more surprised that she'd pay for it out of her own purse.'

Another pause. This time old Fluornoy rocked up and down once. Bonnie wished mightily he'd get on with it. She knew as well as Albert also knew, that he hadn't made this long drive at night just to acquaint them with the fact that the hospital board had met.

'And,' he began again, still enunciating very carefully, 'they'd like first to meet you, Miss Harper; ask you a few questions – then of course sack you.'

Bonnie's breath eased out. She was almost relieved. Albert wasn't, in fact he looked sternly at Doctor Fluornoy and said, 'They'd better sack me too, sir. Better still, I'll appear before them at the same time and *resign!*'

Fluornoy didn't appear ruffled. 'That's your prerogative,' he said soberly. 'In any case they'd like to see all three of us promptly at ten in the morning in my office. That's why I drove up here tonight. To make certain you'd be there. I tried telephoning but neither home appeared to have anyone in it.' He looked out over their heads again.

'I can understand why now, of course.' He looked down again. 'Well; that's all. I'll be heading on back now. Sorry to have interrupted.'

On the spur of the moment Bonnie stepped over and held up her hand. The diamond still shone with that fierce blue fire. Old Fluornoy looked, bent for a closer inspection, then straightened back up.

'Very beautiful, Miss Harper. But then for a girl who is also strikingly beautiful a young man could scarcely do less, eh Doctor Heath?'

Albert muttered something and turned to follow the older man and Bonnie back up out of the garden. His face was finally set in the stubborn cast of a man angry enough about something to fight.

CHAPTER TWELVE

At ten o'clock the following morning Bonnie was deep in ward-work. She asked Miss Cummings if she'd telephone upstairs and make an excuse, saying Bonnie would be slightly late.

Miss Cummings returned with a pale face and round eyes. 'You'd better go up right now,' she said. 'I got Doctor Fluornoy instead of his secretary. He wasn't in his best mood.'

There was nothing for it but to go. She told Miss Cummings what she wanted done and how to do it. She also looked her assistant straight in the eye and said, 'I telephoned into the city for flowers this morning, Helen. When they arrive please see that they're apportioned so that each patient has a few on his bedstand.'

Cummings faintly nodded. 'Flowers, Miss Harper...?'

Bonnie smiled sweetly, didn't answer, turned and marched out of Ward B.

She felt queasy riding to the third floor but after leaving the lift she almost felt panicky. The corridor was long, glistening, well-lighted and empty. Walking down it to Doctor Fluornoy's office was like walking The Last Mile.

She turned where a window was inset in the massive wall, stopped and stood looking out over the city, out over the distant ocean, for several moments sternly scolding herself. They couldn't really fire her because she had a typed resignation in her pocket which she'd hand to Doctor Fluornoy's secretary the moment she entered his office.

What, then, was there to be so panicky about?

Albert, she told herself. *He shouldn't have to leave Nicholson where he was happy, simply because of her – and his love of her.*

'Miss Harper...'

She turned, Doctor Fluornoy's handsome, poised secretary was gazing at her from a doorway, slightly perplexed. Bonnie turned, gave herself one last stern admonition, felt much better, and marched straight over, dug out the resignation, wordlessly handed it to Miss Singleton – and felt still better so she smiled.

Miss Singleton, holding the envelope, said, 'All the others are inside.'

Bonnie opened the intervening door and walked straight into the crowded little office. At once five men sprang up. One was John Fluornoy – wearing his suit coat instead of the ward-coat for a change, another was Albert Heath looking grim as death, and the other three were fleshy, sturdy men, sober as judges, whom Doctor Fluornoy introduced almost indifferently as 'Mister Staunton, Mister Belcher, and Mister Funston.' The way Doctor Fluornoy said those names was almost discourteous, and one of them, Belcher, a loose-lipped, vague-faced man, looked sharply at old Fluornoy.

She acknowledged each name with a prim nod. Then she smiled as the men sat and as Albert Heath gallantly but rather pointlessly held a chair for her.

For five seconds the governing board members looked at one another, at Doctor Fluornoy, and even at Miss Harper. Someone had to start the ball rolling; they were waiting.

Doctor Fluornoy did it, his voice quiet, concise, crisp, his pale eyes looking at some vague spot above Bonnie's head. 'Miss Harper, as you are aware these gentlemen control the hospital's purse-strings. As you are also aware they know of your little – innovations. They'd like to discuss those things with you.'

Before the board members began speaking Bonnie got the distinct feeling that Doctor Fluornoy wasn't at all pleased about any of this. She didn't believe it was simply over the time consumed, which kept him from his work, nor entirely because the board members were making this enquiry; she thought, because she had an idea she knew how Doctor Fluornoy functioned, that he strongly resented interference in his field, which was the dictatorial administration of Nicholson Hospital.

She was exactly right.

Mister Belcher began by asking decently enough if paying for the redecorating of Ward B hadn't been expensive. She said that it had been, but that she'd had the money, had no other particular use for it, and therefore used it where she knew it would do an enormous amount of good.

That gave Mister Funston an opportunity to pounce and he took it. 'Miss Harper; did it occur to you redecorating Ward B wasn't within your authority; that the governing board makes all policy decisions for Nicholson?'

She smiled sweetly at Funston. 'It was such a small thing, Mister Funston, and I realized you gentlemen were all busy businessmen. Believe me, if it had been something really important, I'd have gone to Doctor Fluornoy first.'

Funston looked a little deflated. Mister Staunton, ready to speak, closed his mouth and slowly relaxed in his chair making a close study of Bonnie. This gave Mister Belcher his chance.

In the same polite tone he said, 'Incense,

Miss Harper? Newsboys pelting through the ward as though it were a sports arena? Special care in a ward?'

'And flowers,' said Bonnie, turning her sweetest smile on old Belcher. 'This morning I had a load of freshly cut flowers brought in with orders that they were to be divided so that every patient got a vase of them on his nightstand.'

Belcher looked at his fellows, over at Heath, then finally in silent appeal at Doctor Fluornoy. But that was a mistake. Everyone except perhaps the board members knew how much John Fluornoy liked flowers. So much so in fact that each afternoon he took a book and went among them for an hour.

Belcher said, 'Did you know about the flowers, Doctor?'

Fluornoy acidly smiled. 'No sir I did not. But I think it's a capital idea.'

Funston, Belcher, even quiet Staunton gazed at Fluornoy. He didn't drop his gaze nor did his acid smile atrophy. He said, 'Gentlemen; I have surgery before noon. I'm sure each of you has something to do also. Why don't we just get on with it?'

As though that were a cue Albert Heath soberly fished inside his coat, brought forth

135

a long white envelope and handed it to Mister Belcher, who was sitting closest to him.

Belcher looked from the envelope to Heath. He seemed to know what was inside the envelope. He leaned, carefully placed the envelope before Doctor Fluornoy on the desk and sank back silent.

Bonnie guessed about the envelope's contents too. She said, 'Gentlemen; as for removing me from my position – you needn't bother; I handed my resignation to Doctor Fluornoy's secretary when I entered the office a few minutes ago. But I strongly urge you not to accept a resignation from Doctor Heath.'

Funston, pulling on his upper lip and gazing from Bonnie to Fluornoy, was the first to notice the engagement ring; at least he was the first to appear to attach a significance to it that might be relevant. He finally said, 'Miss Harper; would you object terribly to a personal question?'

She shook her head. 'I'll answer any question I can, sir.'

Funston's eyes turned kindly. 'You are engaged?'

'Yes sir.'

'Ahhh… To Doctor Heath by any chance?'

'Yes sir, to Doctor Heath.'

John Fluornoy said harshly, 'Gentlemen; I suggest we get on with this. The girl's quit and so has Doctor Heath. I'm due in surgery. Is there anything else; would you care to sue her?'

That startled all three board members. 'What for?' Belcher blurted, round-eyed.

'Well hell, gentlemen, *I* don't know,' snapped old Fluornoy, thoroughly out of patience now. *'You* are the governors of Nicholson. Perhaps for defacing public property – painting the blasted walls. Or for burning incense in a public building. There must be a legal statute covering anything as outlandish as that, even though it would make you the laughing stock of the countryside if you used it for grounds. The point I'd like to make is this: you can't sack her because she's quit. If you had in mind rebuking Doctor Heath – it's too late for that also. And as I've repeatedly said, I'm due in surgery.'

The board members heard Fluornoy out gazing straight at him. They didn't seem the least bit embarrassed by his blunt harangue, but all three of them looked a little dubious, as though something unexpected had occurred for which they were not prepared.

Mister Staunton, the quietest one of the three men, eventually said, 'Steady, John. We're only here in the capacity of a board of enquiry.'

Fluornoy looked hard at Staunton. 'Ed, you told me last night you favoured getting rid of Miss Harper. I had half the night and couple of hours this morning to dwell on that.' Fluornoy arose, leaned on his desk and brought up that acid, decidedly unpleasant smile. 'I think I have an ideal solution for you.'

'Good,' enthused Belcher. 'What is it?'

The iceberg-blue eyes swung slowly and rested upon Mister Belcher. 'I quit!'

Bonnie was as stunned as the others all were. Albert stared disbelievingly. Funston stopped pulling on his lip and Mister Belcher very gingerly eased back in his chair. Staunton slowly puckered his eyes nearly closed.

'You don't mean that,' he said softly. 'John; Nicholson has been your life. You put it on a supporting basis. You've run it like–'

'That's precisely the point,' said Fluornoy, diving straight into the opening Staunton had presented him, 'I'm *not* running it. *You* gentlemen are. And since that's the case...' Doctor Fluornoy reared back looking down his nose. '...Run it! Get yourself another man for my place, for Heath's place and for the young lady's position.' He turned and while the others sat silently watching, marched out into the other office, slammed the door behind himself, and left a big vacuum behind.

Staunton cleared his throat and gazed round. Bonnie was watching Albert. He didn't seem to know what to do, which was something he shared with the board members. She also arose.

'Gentlemen, please excuse me. I've a full load in my ward and if there's nothing further here...'

Albert took his cue and stood up looking grim, but if Belcher and Funston were caught off base by all this, John Staunton wasn't – or else he made a very fast recovery, for he said, 'Miss Harper; Doctor Heath; just one moment more.' He smiled, which he seemed to do easily. 'No one has come right out and said the board *disapproved* of the innovations here at Nicholson.' Staunton paused, seemed to search for the words to use next, and finally said, 'Please – give the board a day or two for considering all this. Hold your resignations in abeyance until then, will you?'

Albert, who'd been silent for the most part now asked a question. 'Do you believe Doctor Fluornoy will hold *his* resignation in abeyance?'

Everyone in the room knew old Fluornoy wasn't bluffing; they also knew when he said he was through he didn't mean a week hence, he meant today.

Funston, taking his lead from Staunton's conciliatory attitude, said blandly, 'We'll talk to Doctor Fluornoy. After all he's been here longer than any of us have even been on the governing board. Longer than anyone else. He lives and breathes Nicholson. I think we can get him to come round.'

That sounded so palpably asinine Bonnie couldn't help but offer a quiet retort. 'Gentlemen; I'll agree to stay exactly as long as Doctor Fluornoy stays.' She turned, stepped to the door and turned back when Staunton spoke to her.

'Miss Harper, the board will go into Executive Session right away – today. Just promise you'll do nothing until you've heard from us.'

She took the same view of that remark. 'I've been offered an excellent job – at quite a bit more money, incidentally – at a private sanatorium in the suburbs, gentlemen. If you think I should breathlessly await your decision, I'll have to differ with that.'

She opened the door, stepped through and hastily closed it before any of them could call her back.

Miss Singleton was watching her with shrewd, wise eyes, and a little smile down around her lips. 'Well done,' she said very quietly. 'By the way, Doctor Fluornoy had no surgery this morning. He'll be down in the cafeteria drinking black coffee – his sole dissipation – if you'd care to go down.'

'Why should I?'

'Well,' said Miss Singleton gently, 'he didn't resign simply because they tried to over-ride him, Miss Harper. You *were* involved, you know.'

Bonnie felt ashamed. 'I'm sorry,' she said. 'Of course I'll go down.'

CHAPTER THIRTEEN

When Bonnie appeared at the table where John Fluornoy was sitting hunched around a white crockery mug of black coffee exactly as Miss Singleton had said he'd be, he raised his eyes without moving his head, looked at her a moment then growled.

'If you aren't needed in Ward B, please join me in a cup of bile, Nurse Harper.' Then, as she quietly sat, he said, 'And if you think you have to be grateful or anything ridiculous, please just keep it to yourself.'

She felt better at once. When a waitress appeared she ordered tea. 'That was foolish of you,' she said.

The iceberg-eyes jumped to her face. It had probably been a very long while since anyone had said anything like that to old John Fluornoy, or had used quite that quiet, familiar tone of voice. But he didn't growl and a moment later dropped his eyes to the coffee cup again.

'What is there about one nurse that is important enough for two physicians to resign over, Doctor?'

He snorted. 'One nurse be hanged, young lady. You were only incidental.'

'I know,' she murmured. 'They stepped on your autocratic toes a little.'

'A little?' he snorted, then thought a moment and added: 'Autocratic? My dear Miss Harper, aren't you aware yet that every hospital has one head man; I don't care a hang how many boards of governors or whatever they call themselves a hospital has – it always has *one* chief. At Nicholson for the past–'

'I know Doctor Fluornoy, I know all that. But resigning like that – literally flinging the job in their faces...?'

'How else, may I ask? When a man is certain he is right, let me tell you there's only one thing to do. Make your position unequivocally known!'

'Fine,' she said, leaning away for the waitress to place her cup of tea down. 'But not *the* chief man, Doctor. He's above that kind of thing.'

'Not this one, young lady.'

She sipped the tea, found it just right, and turned as someone approaching from the lift caught her attention. Albert Heath came over, didn't ask if he could sit with them, pulled out a chair and dropped astraddle of it. Bonnie thought of something irrelevant: Miss Singleton. She was indeed a very wise person. Now she had all three of them in the cafeteria.

'Well,' grumped Doctor Fluornoy, shooting Albert a look.

'They're in Executive Session.'

'Right there in my office?' growled old

Fluornoy. 'Confound it this isn't a railroad station.'

Albert looked at Bonnie. 'Who cares?' he asked. 'They can hold a Roman orgy on the rooftop if they choose.'

Fluornoy blinked.

Bonnie smiled at her fiancé. He didn't smile back but he slipped a hand over her fingers atop the table. Fluornoy saw that too – and cleared his throat exactly as he'd done in the garden the night before.

'In that case you'd like a new position,' he said, addressing Albert but looking into his coffee cup. 'There is an excellent opening over at Sydney. I was contacted about it day before yesterday by telephone.'

'And you?' asked Bonnie, switching her attention back to the older man.

'I've been sitting here thinking,' answered Fluornoy. 'At least I *was* thinking about it before this table became a trysting place for young lovers. I think I'll retire. I've some decent investments; I don't *have* to go on peering into chest and abdominal cavities if I don't choose to.' He raised his head looking a lot less bleak, looking almost gentle. 'Raise flowers. Did you know Mrs Fluornoy used to cultivate carnations?'

Neither of them had ever heard anyone,

least of all Doctor Fluornoy, mention the fact, obvious now, that he'd once had a wife.

'She loved them; in fact during the war when I was in Australia, and later on back in the Philippines again, Mrs Fluornoy had some of the finest variegated specimens known. My speciality was roses, of course; always been very partial to roses, you know. Well; perhaps I could divide up a parcel of ground, half to roses, half to carnations.'

Bonnie felt a quick, hard tug at her heartstrings. She'd never before considered Doctor Fluornoy as a person, always as a very successful and prominent surgeon. Now, she saw through the tiny crack in his crusty façade and saw something else – something she'd never guessed had ever existed: a man with a heart full of memories for a woman who had died.

She dropped her head quickly to stir the tea.

Albert was gloomy. 'I don't much favour the idea of Australia,' he told John Fluornoy. 'Perhaps I'd better emigrate to the States – or up to Canada.'

Fluornoy nodded, looking into the coffee cup again. 'At your age I think I'd do the same. Someday this part of the world will be paramount. But for the next twenty years or so I'd risk a guess that it'll just be growing up to that destiny. Of course you're right, Albert; moreover, once married you'll have to make wise decisions. By the way; when *will* you be married?'

They couldn't answer that; they'd only just the night before become engaged. Doctor Fluornoy understood and arose from the table saying he'd better get back upstairs. By now Funston, Belcher and Staunton ought to be out of the building and perhaps he could get on with his work without any additional damnfool interruptions.

Bonnie stopped him. 'Doctor Fluornoy; Mister Belcher said they'd try and get you to re-consider.'

'That was decent of them wasn't it?'

'Sir; they asked me to do the same. I said I'd stay just as long as you did and no longer.'

Fluornoy's glacial gaze almost softened. 'Miss Harper; never hitch your star to someone else's star. Particularly an old man's star. You are young – the whole road is strung out before you.'

'I'll remember the advice, Doctor, but I meant exactly what I said. If you go – I also go.'

Fluornoy finally smiled. 'But you've already resigned.'

Bonnie flushed. 'Well; that was just so they couldn't sack me.'

'Of course it was. But about those innovations – you told me yesterday there'd be no more. But this morning there were flowers weren't there?'

Her blush was darker after that statement. 'Flowers scarcely count, do they, Doctor?'

He shrugged wide, bony shoulders. '*Anything*, Miss Harper. Anything at all is what I meant.'

'If I promise now, Doctor Fluornoy...?' She was looking up at him very seriously, her eyes large, her mouth soft-held.

He blew out a big breath and wryly gazed at Albert. 'Son, I see no end of complications for you with this girl. Look at her; will you tell me how a man with any red blood at all could scold her?'

Albert said nothing; he merely squeezed the small, tan hand he was holding.

Fluornoy thought a moment. He was in a much better mood now than he'd been in when they'd first sat round the table.

'I'll do some thinking,' he said, and after nodding curtly went striding off in the direction of the lift.

Bonnie waited until he was gone then raised her brows in enquiry, but Albert had no answer. 'I wouldn't bet either way,' he said. 'And if I know him at all he won't tell anyone either, not even the board. He'll either be here in the morning as crusty as ever – or he won't be.'

'And us, Albert?'

He slowly smiled. 'You were dead right last night. Nicholson *does* interfere, doesn't it?'

She returned to Ward B shortly after she and Albert parted in the cafeteria. The first person she encountered was her assistant, Helen Cummings. But Cummings was too tactful to ask direct questions and since Bonnie actually had no set answers she couldn't volunteer anything. That's how it stood between them.

But the second person she encountered, Mister McCann, reacted differently. He called her over, squinted his small, shrewd eyes and said, 'There are all manner of rumours flying about this morning, Miss Harper. I just want an answer from you about one of them: did the governing board go after you a bit for these flowers and some of the other things?'

She said, 'A bit, Mister McCann,' and managed to escape before he asked any more questions.

The Japanese seaman's friends had been in during visiting hours. They were gone by the time Bonnie got up that far among the patients so she hardly expected what happened.

The sailor smiled at her approach. He looked quite good considering he'd had surgery so short a while before. She greeted him then stopped a moment to take his pulse when he brought forth something from beneath the covers and held it out to her. It was a small box looking slightly the worse for wear. She took it automatically but when she looked inside and saw the ghostly shine of a solitary very large pearl she at once closed the box.

The seaman's dark, unreadable eyes clung to her face. He said, 'For you. I bring for my wife in Japan. But now for you.'

She tried to get him to take back the valuable gift. He steadfastly declined. She pleaded. He simply refused. There really was no way she could reason with the man; his knowledge of English, while quite understandable, was obviously limited. He seemed to *know* a fair amount, but had to plot each short sentence well in advance before delivering it. Under those circumstances all he had to do to win his argument was grin, shake his head, and refuse to take back the small box. Finally, he explained.

'I die here, my wife no need pearl from dead husband. She need *live* husband. All right. You make husband... You make *me* try to live. So ... my *wife* really give you pearl. Now you see?'

Bonnie 'saw'. She also felt a lump in her throat. She thanked the seaman softly, finished taking his pulse and moved on, still with the lump in her throat. She thought of getting the man's address in Japan from his admission records, then mailing the pearl to his wife. But of course that wouldn't sit well with the sailor. He very definitely wanted Bonnie to have that pearl.

Later, when she returned to the office in late afternoon, she had it in her pocket. She transferred it to her street clothes and temporarily forgot about it while bringing some records current. After that, Mister McCann sent word he'd like to see her. She didn't go. Instead, she sent Helen Cummings, then, before Cummings could come back with the inevitable reply, Bonnie walked out into the corridor – and came face to face with Doctor Bryan, the new intern in charge of Administration. She nodded coolly to his quick, avid smile, and because the only escape route left was straight ahead, she strode across and entered Ward A.

She could see Sampson down there, propped up and volubly talking to several other patients, who were all hanging on every word. She could guess without much difficulty what Sampson was telling the others, and whom she was speaking about. That was mildly distressing, so Bonnie waited until she was certain Doctor Bryan was gone, turned and walked out into the corridor.

It was a mistake. Doctor Bryan *wasn't* gone. He threw her a roguish wink and sauntered over. 'I don't have anything contagious,' he said. 'The least a pretty girl could do would be volunteer to show a perfect stranger about the city's nightlife – like perhaps tonight?'

She used that very sweet and very disarming smile, raised the engagement ring and said, 'I'll ask Doctor Heath. If he's willing, I'll be glad to show you round, Doctor Bryan.'

He got off a clumsy apology and fled.

When Bonnie went back to change into street clothes it was a half hour after the normal time for her shift to be gone. She managed to change and escape before any of the night nurses cornered her. They certainly would have heard she'd been up before the board in Doctor Fluornoy's office this day.

She made a clean escape, got outside and was heading away from the hospital when a man in a shiny auto cruised up from behind very slowly, leaned out and said, with a leer, 'Going my way, lady?'

Every muscle tightened. Every nerve grew taut. She turned. It was Albert. His leer slid away and he laughed at the cold, fierce look on her face.

She had to wait a second or two for the anger to diminish otherwise she might have said something she didn't mean. She utilized that time by going round to get into the car beside him.

Then she said, 'I'm not really terribly surprised. The first people I was warned against after I graduated from nursing school were the doctors.'

He still chuckled. 'You looked ready to freeze me to the bone.'

Finally, she laughed too, then he headed for the mountainside roadway through a failing, warm day.

152

CHAPTER FOURTEEN

Bonnie called home to tell Beth she and Albert Heath were having dinner uptown. They went to that same restaurant they'd visited on their first night out together but this time there was no redhead to distract either of them and the food, while not exceptional at all, was, as Bonnie analysed it, substantial, solid, nourishing. She made a note of that; evidently Albert's tastes didn't run to exotic foods, which was just as well because Bonnie had never learned much about cooking. She was a career girl, or at least had always considered herself one.

After dinner they drove along the sea-shore. Nicholson seemed very far away. For the matter of that everything except each other seemed far away. There wasn't as much heavenly co-operation as there'd been several days back – the moon was nearly gone – but they didn't need it now as much either.

He took her to a promontory where they could look outward upon the steel sea or

153

turn a bit and look down across the city, nestling in its large mountain-girt cove. In another direction stood the spiny hills with high, bent ridges, brushed-off slopes and skeletal silhouettes.

He said he'd once been brought to this spot by a man who dealt in land who wished to sell the promontory to him. 'There was a small drawback: no water.' He turned, motioning with one arm. 'Community water pipes don't reach within a mile of the place.'

'So you didn't buy it. Very practical, Albert.'

'No. No, love. I *did* buy it.'

'Without water?'

He looked out over the sea. 'As a matter of fact the way the city's expanding it'll only be a matter of perhaps three, four years before the water system is extended nearby, and meanwhile I'll come up here and feed my soul on the view.' He gazed at her. 'Not practical, I'll admit, but terribly satisfying.'

The idea of a home atop this fabulously scenic spot intrigued her. In fact, never having had a home, not even as a child except in the rented category, the longer she dwelt upon outright ownership of a residence atop the knoll the more thrilling the notion appeared.

She said, 'I love it, Albert,' and strolled out an acre or so to gaze down where the beach curved round the solid granite base like a broad band of hammered silver.

He stood watching her. There was just enough starlight to limn her against the dark background. She was lithe and wholesome with a healthy glow. In his opinion she was very desirable and extremely attractive. He walked out to her.

'Something Doctor Fluornoy said today...'

She turned. 'Yes, I know... Well; when *shall* we get married?'

He laughed. 'Very good. That's ideal perception. I'm not at all sure I'd want you reading my mind all the time, but in this case I like it.'

She responded to his laughter with a light mood. 'Albert, you'd be surprised how often a woman can read a man's mind. Of course as we were taught in school, the basic drives are paramount therefore–'

'Delightful,' he murmured wryly. 'Exactly why I brought you up here tonight – a nursing school lecture on fundamental biology.'

She leaned, kissed him squarely on the lips as he finished speaking then spun away before he recovered and threw out his arms, and walked back towards the mid-point of their hilltop. He followed.

'It's your decision,' he said, reverting to what they'd been discussing. 'Too late for a June wedding of course.'

She turned impish eyes upon him. 'We could wait until next June.'

He nodded. 'We could. Then again we could be married tomorrow.'

'Hardly tomorrow, Albert. I've a full schedule in Ward B – providing I'm still allowed in there tomorrow. I keep trying to solve the riddle of John Fluornoy: will he or will he not, return?'

Albert flapped both arms and rolled up his eyes. 'You want to discuss the perils of Pauline when I'm trying to marry you.'

She smiled. 'Next Friday afternoon?'

He affected bewilderment. 'Do you mean Doctor Fluornoy may not return until next–'

'You know perfectly well what I mean, Albert Heath!'

'Oh. You mean *marriage*. Well that's terribly considerate of you, Miss Harper. And yes, next Friday afternoon will do quite nicely. I'll make a note of it on my calendar.'

'I wouldn't want to crowd you, Doctor. We

could wait until the—'

He lunged, she dodged, and they both laughed. The lamps of a cruising automobile diverted them long enough for him to say their promontory was actually a somewhat popular spot with young couples out driving. They watched the car creep closer, then veer off. Evidently the driver had seen Albert's auto up there.

They returned to the car, switched on the radio and sat a moment listening to some crisp, grim newscaster, then he punched a button and music came forth. He put an arm across the back of the seat touching her shoulders, her hair. She eased her head back, turned her face to him and waited. He bent to kiss her and she came up to meet him.

Afterwards he murmured words to the effect that before she'd come along he'd almost given up. 'I looked. Never doubt that. After all when a man passes the thirty-year milestone he has reason to look; if he hopes to have a family he'd best be about it. But – it's difficult to explain – there are pretty girls, educated, sophisticated, poised and worldly girls, even rich girls – or at least girls whose fathers are rich – but none of them ever measured up for some reason.'

She lay there waiting for more. She liked him best when he was close to her, quiet and thoughtful. He had it in him to be fiery; she knew that from several of his kisses. She also knew other things about him; that he was very loyal, for example – witness what he'd done that afternoon when the board of governors had meant to fire her from Nicholson – and he was strong enough to stand up for his convictions.

But when she felt most secure with him was when he was calm and pensive, as he was now, his voice soft, his words sound, his candour coming straight from the heart.

'It seemed as though you'd never come along, Bonnie I'd just about given up.'

She'd heard many times that if a man avoids marriage until he's past thirty he's likely to avoid it permanently. Or else that he was likely to become too particular, too critical. At twenty she couldn't say with any certainty how a *woman* felt after thirty, but she knew herself well enough to realize she'd never have been satisfied with spinsterhood. She said, 'You might be too anxious, Albert, too vulnerable.'

To keep the conversation from becoming morbid, evidently, he said lightly, 'Vulnerable or not, duck, I'll never be bored. In fact, I'd never know from day to day what colour the parlour walls might be, or where I'd find flowers.'

She turned her head a little to catch the twinkle in his eyes. 'Did you know you are quite handsome?'

'Yes of course,' he said. 'Did you just notice?'

She laughed and reached for him, thrilling to an indefinable happiness. His humour was likely to crop up at any time; she liked that. Her first view of him had half inclined her to believe he might be too serious, too dedicated in his profession to possess much humour.

'Not really,' she said, holding him. 'I only said that to bolster your ego. Actually, you're ugly as sin.'

He kissed her, brushed her lips with his mouth and lay her head upon his shoulder. 'It's this poor light,' he said. 'In bright daylight I turn into a veritable Prince Charming. Which reminds me; did you know John Fluornoy had been married?'

She shook her head drowsily. Right at that moment she didn't really care. 'No.'

'Nor did I. But this evening as I was leaving I rode down in the lift with his secretary. I mentioned it. She said his wife died shortly after the war – right here in New Zealand – which is why he's remained here ever since. She also told me something else. Did you realize he was a Kentish man?'

The way he said it made it sound like a Neanderthal Man or a Cro-Magnon man. She didn't answer. It made her melancholy anyway, thinking of Doctor Fluornoy and right at the moment she didn't want to feel that way.

'Where will we live?' she asked, looking up at him.

'Oh. Yes; that *is* important isn't it? Well; I've very nice rooms in a hotel.'

'Albert!'

He looked down then away again. 'Yes. It doesn't sound very thrilling does it? How about pitching a tent beside the sea?'

'Or right here on your promontory.'

'Sarcasm doesn't become you. You're entirely too beautiful and fragile.'

She blinked, never having thought of herself as fragile. Nor, for the matter of that, was she fragile. Lithe, yes, but not fragile. She had the constitution of a horse, the endurance of a bear and the health as Doctor Fluornoy had facetiously observed, of two strong people.

'A cottage,' she murmured. 'Not too far

from the seashore?'

He nodded. 'Exactly what I was going to suggest.'

'When is your next free day from the hospital?'

He thought a moment. 'Any time, really. I resigned, don't you remember?'

'You didn't mean it any more than I did.'

He looked at her. 'No, I really didn't. But I've enough time logged to take a day off if I wish.'

'Day after tomorrow?'

'Why not tomorrow?'

'Well; I've a swarm of work to do tomorrow.'

'Day after tomorrow it is, then.'

They sealed it with a kiss. The music came softly from the car wireless, the night's warmth and faint fragrance lay all round and overhead a veritable sea of stars cast gold-dusty light earthward to faintly brighten their private world.

'Beth and Charles don't know,' she told him, leaning away just a little and gazing up at him. 'They'll want to do something for us.'

'No need for that, Bonnie.'

'But they'll want to. Beth is the only relative I have.'

He capitulated at once. 'Of course. Whatever you'd like.'

They were close, the music was soporific, and their ecstasy held them quiet for a while. She was acutely conscious of him where they touched at thigh and shoulder. He was muscular, tanned and virile. She could feel the tug of her desire, guessed he would feel the same thing, and where before, when she even sensed that in a companion, her intuitive defences had arisen, with him there was no need. No need at all. *That* she instinctively felt, was *real* love.

Another cruising auto approached and it too veered off at the sight of Albert's car atop the hill. Far out at sea a ghostly vessel ablaze with lights silently sliced through an inky ocean, its motion southward at what seemed a very slow crawl.

He quietly said, 'A house by the sea. A wife.' He rolled his head to look at her profile. 'It seems like a dream.'

She understood that feeling perfectly, except that her heart swelled with the full knowledge that it wasn't a dream, that it was just round the corner for them both.

'I'll really resign, of course.'

He was silent for a while turning that over

in his mind. Ultimately he said, 'Is that what you want, or is it what you think you should do?'

Right there, with him beside her in the night, it was what she wanted. But she forced herself to be forthright too; she was trained in her profession, was good at it, liked it, and was currently engaged in trying to prove that her ideas of what *good* nursing entailed wasn't simply keeping patients properly medicated and solaced.

'Both,' she had to say. 'Perhaps in some jobs working women can be wife and professional simultaneously. I don't see how that can hold true with nursing. Sometimes I don't get away until six or seven at night.' She looked over at him. 'You wouldn't want to look at a tired wife every night, Albert. It wouldn't be fair.'

He said, 'We'll think about it, talk about it.' Then, leaning to find her lips he also said, 'Anyway, there's the possibility that something might come along that would keep you fully enough occupied at home.'

She understood exactly what he meant and kissed him very tenderly because she too wanted that very much.

CHAPTER FIFTEEN

When she finally arrived at home Beth and Charles were having a nightcap of tea in the kitchen. The moment she stepped through the doorway Beth saw the engagement ring.

'Oh darling,' Beth said, in a tone of voice that was half sad, half glad.

Charles, not following this interplay at once, looked perplexedly at his wife. Beth pointed out the ring, and Charles soberly gazed at it, then up at Bonnie's radiant face.

'Doctor Heath...?'

Bonnie nodded.

Charles ruminated, then said, 'Sound profession, medicine. Good income, excellent prospects for the long haul. Congratulations, Bonnie.'

The following morning in Ward B of course the news had travelled more swiftly, but then others had seen the ring the day before. In fact, although Bonnie had no inkling, everyone at Nicholson had heard of the engagement between Doctor Heath and the controversial young Ward Nurse on the second floor.

Perhaps, if Bonnie *hadn't* been so controversial, all she'd have received would have been congratulations, but as things stood now there was a sharp division of opinion. Not among the patients, especially, nor even among the more progressive members of staff, but there were just enough hard-nosed ultra-conservatives of Elvira Sampson's kind to ensure lively argument.

It was said Bonnie would make Doctor Heath a wonderful wife. It was also said she'd drive him to drink with her unpredictability, with her penchant for change and innovation. Mister McCann, annoyed by something one of the older nurses hinted at, said he'd a damned sight rather be bewildered by a wife than bored to death.

Bonnie, at first unaware of all this, naturally, since like all gossip, she'd be the last to hear any of it, had to force herself to concentrate on her ward; she'd catch herself drifting off into daydreams from time to time.

She did remember one thing, however; she called Miss Singleton on the third floor the first free moment to ask whether or not Doctor Fluornoy had come in. He had, Miss Singleton said, because there'd been a bad auto accident the night before and he'd been the most qualified surgeon, so the hospital had got him out of bed. He was in his office in fact, and Miss Singleton said if Bonnie would like she'd switch the call to him. Bonnie hadn't wanted that at all; she'd only wished to make certain he was there.

She saw Albert twice that morning, once the length of the corridor where he was in conversation with two other doctors, and again when he'd made a quick examination of the Japanese seaman. But both times she'd been in a hurry so all they'd managed had been a long, long exchange of looks.

Two men arrived an hour ahead of proper visiting hours asking to see Mister McCann at once, explaining they were city officials and didn't wish to trade on this fact, but simply could not get back at the correct time. She took them into Ward B and pointed the way to McCann's bed, then quite forgot the men because she had three new admittees to look after, two from the same auto collision Doctor Fluornoy had been involved with, and the third new patient was a policeman who'd got himself struck down from behind while trying to break up a brawl in some tenderloin night-club. The policeman was a jolly, rueful individual, very large and outgoing. He confessed to a mild headache, but when she would have ordered treatment for a fractured skull he said no, he'd been thoroughly gone over the night before – even to having been X-rayed – and that his injury was more of the pride than the head. She got him some headache pills and went to look at the other people. They were badly cut up but what ailed both of them more than anything else was shock. They were both young men and wanted to know the fate of their friend, upon whom Doctor Fluornoy had had to operate.

She called upstairs, got this information and took it back to them. Their friend'd lost his left leg below the knee. It was a terrible thing to have to say, but she sent down to the medical library on the first floor for books on artificial limbs and told them to bone up. 'It's not nearly as bad as it used to be. Don't take my word for it. Read what the books say.'

Shortly before noon a small, very sober-faced middle-aged man from the Japanese consulate called to make enquiries about the sailor. She let him read the chart, told him the seaman was making wonderful progress, then, although again in violation of visiting-hours rules, took the diplomat up to see his countryman.

She got a belated lunch then hastened straight back. The Japanese diplomat was waiting very patiently in her tiny office. He arose at once when she entered, bowed and smiled at her. He had been educated, he told her, in England; had learned great respect for the English and their institutions, and had waited simply to tell her that his injured countryman's glowing reports of his treatment at Nicholson – especially his care at Miss Harper's hands – would go to his home government; that he was personally very impressed by the individual attention given patients of Ward B and would consider it a great honour if he might be permitted to bring some Japanese doctors who would be shortly visiting New Zealand, to see her ward.

She was surprised. She was also flustered. She said she'd be delighted to have the gentlemen visit Ward B, but that actual permission would have to come from Doctor Fluornoy, who was head-surgeon. The diplomat thanked her, bowed again and departed, bound for Fluornoy's office on the third floor.

She might have felt a little thrill of

pleasure at this recognition, even though it came from foreigners, of her efforts to change Ward B into a place where ill people would rally better and faster, except that she got a call from Ward A, from a nurse named Sanderson whom she did not know, asking if she could spare a moment and come over.

As it turned out Miss Sanderson was the new Ward Nurse. Bonnie hadn't heard anything of the former Ward Nurse leaving Nicholson, but Miss Sanderson said it had been no secret, that her predecessor had accepted a much more remunerative position as Ward Nurse at a local private sanatorium, had given notice two weeks previous, and that the day before had been her last official duty-day.

What Miss Sanderson, who was a large, rawboned, alert, amiable woman, wanted to know, was what colour Bonnie thought would look best on the ward walls and ceiling, and which complementing trim would be best for windows, doors and cupboards.

Bonnie was nonplussed. She knew that Elvira Sampson was a patient of Ward A, and although she'd deliberately avoided looking towards Sampson's bed, she guessed that Sampson would be rancorously watching her right this minute. But more than that, she knew Miss Sanderson didn't dare have her ward repainted. Bonnie'd taken the staff by surprise when *she'd* done that, but there was no chance it could be accomplished again.

She said, 'Has it been authorized, Miss Sanderson?'

The larger, older woman's gunmetal-grey eyes turned wry. 'Not exactly, Miss Harper, but you'll admit you established a precedent. And look at the place. Drab, dead-white, depressingly impersonal... I slipped in and looked at your ward. It's positively home-like. The morale is better than any I've ever seen and I've been in this profession twenty-five years. Now I was wondering – wouldn't want to adopt your colour schemes, you know – so how would a pale sea-blue-green do on the walls with a darker shade on the ceiling, with perhaps a dark green trim?'

Bonnie fidgeted. She didn't understand it, exactly, but she was in the exact position every rebel eventually finds herself – or himself. Having triumphed, the rebel then must consolidate all gains, encourage conviction among all followers, and resist further change, which of course changes them into conservatives.

She also felt a stab of shame for which there was no immediate explanation, but which she knew, once she'd returned to Ward B, was because the precedent she'd established was going to become endemic throughout Nicholson, and that without any question, was going to make it difficult for her, the originator of all this, but it was also going to make it difficult for Doctor Fluornoy who right at the moment had enough troubles of his own.

She escaped from Ward A as quickly as she could, saying only that she agreed with the colour scheme, but that she felt Miss Sanderson should first take it up with Doctor Bryan, administrative head, or perhaps directly with Doctor Fluornoy.

She didn't realize how late it was until, shortly past three o'clock, she returned from the drug room where she'd gone in response to a call from Helen Cummings, and saw her patients reading their daily papers.

She paused a moment in the upper far doorway surveying her ward, and felt pride. The room *was* appealing. It was also airy and fresh with the fragrance of flowers throughout. She *was* pleased with it, and yet when she dwelt upon the discord all this had caused, it also made her melancholy.

She shook off that mood and started on down towards the little office. Several of her ward nurses were busy. Two turned to throw smiles her way. Another one made it a point to be close by when Bonnie moved through so she could get a close-up view of the ring. That particular girl's face shown with candid envy; she too was young, but beyond that, unfortunately, there wasn't much comparison.

Helen Cummings brought round some mail and Bonnie, who had forgot those men who'd come in earlier to see Mister Mc-Cann, thought of them only momentarily as she passed McCann's bed. For once, he didn't call her over; he simply nodded at her as she swept past, and smiled. She didn't heed the smile especially or she might have had an uneasy moment. McCann still wore that hard little smile after she'd gone past.

Doctor Bryan called before four o'clock to say he'd just admitted an elderly heart case; that as soon as the admittance procedures were completed the patient would be along.

Bonnie had bed space, told one of the nurses to make the assignment, and decided to go down to the cafeteria for a cup of tea.

Actually, since she'd only seen Albert twice this day and neither time close enough to speak to, she was secretly hoping he might be in the cafeteria. But he wasn't.

Someone else was down there though: Miss Singleton. She beckoned and pushed out a chair at her table. She was drinking coffee, and at Bonnie's glance she said it was a vice she'd learned from Doctor Fluornoy.

They sat a moment. Bonnie ordered her tea then Miss Singleton said, 'No word from the board yet.'

Bonnie wasn't very concerned. 'Did Doctor Fluornoy stay on after his early surgery this morning?'

Miss Singleton nodded. 'He's been going over some statistical reports in his office. I think he's writing something.' She smiled. 'He called me to ask how to spell schizhoid. I wasn't sure.' The smile lingered, but the calm, cool eyes were grave. 'It wouldn't seem right around here without him. At least it wouldn't to me, so I typed up my resignation this morning. It's on the desk. I came down here to feel sorry for myself. I've been with him so long, Miss Harper...'

Bonnie felt the same twinge of pain she'd felt for Doctor Fluornoy when he'd been speaking of his wife. She said, 'How can people like that Funston and Belcher and Staunton, with no professional knowledge whatsoever, decide when a great surgeon and a potentially great hospital should stop being great?'

Miss Singleton's little smile was soft, almost wistful, as she answered. 'Checks and balances, my dear. That's how freedom works in a hospital, in a democracy, in life, I suppose. I'll admit I was indignant too for a while, but as Doctor Fluornoy once said, no one who holds the power of life and death in his hands should be allowed to also make mundane decisions.'

Bonnie wasn't quite sure what that meant but it sounded very profound. It also sounded exactly like something John Fluornoy would say. She wondered just for a moment whether Albert would also be a wise, observant surgeon when *he* was John Fluornoy's age.

Miss Singleton changed the subject. 'I understand you and Doctor Heath are to be married very soon. I'm very happy for both of you, Bonnie.'

Miss Singleton had never before used Bonnie's first name. It made a lump settle in the younger woman's throat. There had been a definite drag of soft wistfulness in

Miss Singleton's voice.

'Next Friday,' she answered. 'Tomorrow we're going to see if we can't find a cottage somewhere near the seashore.'

Miss Singleton nodded. 'Exactly the place, the seashore,' then she pushed away her cup, turned brisk and arose. 'I must be getting back. He may want to know how to spell some other word.'

CHAPTER SIXTEEN

When Bonnie got home that night she was dog-tired. She couldn't remember having been so tired before. It wasn't the work, she thrived on that, so it had to be the undercurrents, the tensions, the hour-by-hour drain of her nervous energy rather than her physical energy.

When Charles brought a highball to the verandah where she was sitting in the dusk with Beth, she thanked him with strong feeling. She needed a pick-me-up.

She'd told Beth her plans. Beth relayed them to Charles and he came up with a casual remark that brought Bonnie to the edge of her chair, highball still untouched.

'Quite a coincidence, this cottage by the sea. We are handling an estate with two such cottages. One up in the country a few miles, the other right here in the city.'

Bonnie asked breathlessly if they could be rented. Charles thought they could be, although both actually were to be sold to settle the estate. 'I'll find out in the morning,' he said, and fished for a pen and paper upon which he scribbled both addresses. 'Go look at them,' he said, handing over the paper. 'They may not be anything you'd want anyway, but the idea crossed my mind when you mentioned cottages near the seashore.'

Later, when she was in her own room, she studied the addresses trying to place the houses, but because she actually wasn't very well acquainted despite the fact that she'd been almost a year in the area, she had to give it up.

She slept like a log and the following morning when Albert arrived he and Beth had a cup of tea before Bonnie was presentable. Beth was pleased about the engagement; she wouldn't talk about anything else even after Bonnie came forth. By the time Albert was ready to leave with

Bonnie on the house-hunting expedition, Beth had got out of them just as much as they knew of their plans, which, as Albert mentioned while driving down off the hill, wasn't very much although Beth had made it seem as though it were.

He knew where the city cottage was and drove directly to it. It faced the seashore. In fact it was on a piece of raised ground which gave it an unimpaired view of the beach and also of the endless ocean beyond. But there were other homes up close on both sides, and down across the intervening distance towards the seashore rooftops marched in tumbled disarray.

The cottage itself was pleasant, airy, not very old and in a citified way, very charming. But when Albert said he'd settle for it, Bonnie suggested they drive up and look at the other one.

The second cottage was for them; they both knew it almost before he'd stopped the car. It was alone upon its little sidehill with a weed-choked little private road leading to it. Someone had spent many hours planting a lovely garden, drying up now and weedy from neglect. Bonnie found a sprinkler and set it to watering the parched flowers and shrubbery before she went inside.

The entire front wall was one large, thick glass window. There were wooden shutters to close if a gale blew inward from the sea, and there was nothing to distract from their view, which was breathtakingly spectacular.

The parlour was a large room with a low, timbered ceiling. The fireplace had been made of native stone and showed the dark stains of good use. The other rooms were airy, pleasant, but not very large. But above all else, there was something indefinable about the cottage. It seemed to have stored up someone's happiest memories. The windows sparkled from sunlight, a little sea-breeze played in treetops out back and the stone-floored front porch was peacefully shaded from every angle.

Albert made a man's inspection of rafters, footings, attic, garage out back, and said he thought someone had built the cottage over a period of time by himself. It had personal touches, such as the Dutch doors leading outside, in front and back, the leaded windows in the two bedrooms, the sunken tub in the bath and the rather extensive stone work out back in the garden where terraced earth had been painstakingly levelled to make room for the profusion of flowers and bushes.

He finally asked her, when they'd completed their inspection and were standing in the perpetual shadow of the front verandah, if she liked it.

She turned and said, 'Albert, I *love* it. I've never had such a feeling about a house before. Whoever he was, whatever memories he left here, have gone to make exactly the atmosphere a home should have.'

He smiled. There was a look of complete understanding on his face. 'A place far enough out, yet not too far,' he agreed, 'with peace and quiet. I doubt even the dream house I've had in mind since buying the promontory would have this atmosphere.' He paused, then said, 'Let's buy it.'

Buying the cottage hadn't occurred to her. It took a moment for the possibility to sink in. She'd never lived in a house of her own. Even as a child, even while living with Beth who was her own sister, she'd never had that feeling of belonging which is what it takes to make a person cherish a home. But now, with the possibility very distinct, very plausible, all the pent-up longing came out.

'I have some left,' she said, meaning money but not saying that because she was rushing ahead with her thoughts, temporarily cutting him out of them. 'I spent a good deal at the hospital, of course, but I'd probably have enough left for...'

She saw the look on his face and stopped speaking. He was gazing at her in mild surprise. She wasn't sure whether that was because she'd cut him out, had thought by herself, for herself, as she'd been in the habit of doing as a single girl, or whether that odd look was because he was seeing her excited for the first time.

'I'm sorry,' she said. 'The idea just overwhelmed me. I've never really belonged to a house before.'

He hadn't either, as it turned out, but he put it differently. 'It's farther from Nicholson than is best, I suppose, from the standpoint of commuting. But on the other hand the air is fresher, the silences deeper, the environment more invigorating. The drive back and forth would be like going to the place where a person really belonged.'

He took her hand, walked round back where the sprinkler had put dew on everything, stopped and sniffed of the musty, damp air.

'Carnations,' he murmured. 'I know absolutely nothing about them – or any flower for that matter – but I've always loved their spicy scent. And look at the old rose bushes.'

180

'Do you know anything about weeding?' she asked, gazing round. 'And what cures the backaches that'll come from making all this beautiful again?'

He pulled her close. They stood in shade for a long time, each with an arm around the other, it was softly still out back. Eventually they returned to the house, went through the rooms more leisurely discussing the kind of furnishings they'd need, then went back to the porch with its shade, its cool stone flagging, its peeled log uprights supporting the overhanging broad roof.

'I'll call your brother-in-law at his office,' he told her. 'I wonder what they'd say if I tried for another day off tomorrow?'

She knew the answer to that as well as he did. 'They'd say – No!'

He shrugged. 'All right; suppose we leave a little early for the next week or so, then, and go round looking up furniture?'

She was agreeable. In fact right at that moment if he'd suggested running all the way down to the surf and plunging in, she'd have been agreeable.

They still had half the day left. On the slow drive back to the city she suggested they go straight away and see Charles. 'Or call him first to make certain he's at his office.'

They altered that plan just a little. They went instead to look at furniture in the heart of the city, made notes of the things they'd need, and what they saw that they wanted, then, with the afternoon waning, dropped round to his favourite café for a late luncheon or an early supper, whichever it might have qualified as, and finally drove up the Hamiltons' hill to visit a short while with Beth – tell her of their discovery – and await Charles's arrival to talk about buying the country cottage.

Charles arrived home a little late. Held up, he explained to them on the verandah, by an overwrought client who seemed to believe the time and schedule of a lawyer were without equivocation at the disposal of the public.

That made Albert squirm and later, after Charles'd had his highball and Beth mentioned the cottage, Albert quickly said it wasn't that important; that he'd come round during working hours and see Charles at his office.

Bonnie and Beth stared at him. He finally said, 'Well; I apologize for bringing it up like this, when you're trying to relax at home, but Bonnie and I'd like to know if we can buy that cottage up-country you sent us to see?'

Charles didn't consider the mixing of business and pleasure, evidently, for all he said was, 'Buy it? I thought you simply wanted to rent something for a while. And why that cottage; why not the one in the city. Much handier to everything.'

Bonnie and Albert simply waited for the words to end, meanwhile they sat together gazing straight at Charles. He noticed that. He also saw his wife watching him, and whether he knew the younger couple well enough to read their expressions or not, he most certainly *did* know his wife that well. He finished his drink, set the glass aside and said, 'Quite,' as though something had been said to him. 'Well; of course that cottage up there can be bought. I just can't say yet for how much. There'll have to be an appraisal first. You realize we only just got this estate; it'll take a bit of time to process everything.'

'But couldn't we move in, Charles?' Bonnie wanted to know. 'We've said we'd buy the cottage.'

'It wouldn't be proper,' Charles answered. 'Anyway, the appraisal can't take more than a week or ten...' Charles's words trailed off. He seemed to remember something. 'But of course you'll be getting married within the week, won't you, and will want the cottage a bit before then.' He arose to enter the house. 'Excuse me a moment. I'll make a telephone call.'

Beth placidly smiled as her husband disappeared inside. She didn't say as much, but she had unshakable confidence in Charles. 'He'll take care of things,' was all she said.

Albert absently nodded. He said to Bonnie, 'Now, I'm beginning to flinch at thought of the cost. If the owner knows someone wants the place – well – you know how human nature works.'

Bonnie reached to squeeze his hand.

Charles returned much sooner than any of them expected. He said he'd tried to reach his partner by telephone and had failed, but that he *had* reached the appraiser who had promised to go round first thing in the morning and look at the cottage. He would then have his report on Charles's desk by noon.

'So if you two would care to join me for luncheon tomorrow I'd have the information for you.'

Doctor Heath smiled his gratitude then said, 'Since your wife will be interested also, Bonnie and I'll come for her in the car and the three of us will meet you.'

Charles was perfectly agreeable; he just didn't seem to realize that otherwise he'd left his wife out. Of course his wife had recognized it, and after Albert's offer her doe-like eyes rested serenely upon him. Doctor Heath had just demonstrated a degree of consideration for others that had made Beth Hamilton a strong admirer of his.

Bonnie took Albert down into the garden where they had a private view of the city while Beth went inside to feed her husband. They both had invited Albert and Bonnie to join them, but neither of the younger couple felt hungry. They'd had that very late luncheon or 'high tea' whichever it was.

There was some kind of celebration in process far out along the oceanside promenade; fireworks exploded out over the water in every colour and a number of docked ships had their lights blazing from stem to stern. It was very impressive to see, and to watch, from the distant elevation of the Hamiltons' garden.

But it was very difficult to concentrate upon. Albert said, 'Duck, I'm beginning to get cold feet. I've been thinking of all manner of wretched things which could happen.'

She gave him a tender look, leaned and kissed his cheek. 'Does that help any?' she asked.

He thought a moment then smiled. 'Odd about that. Now I can't remember any of the things I was worrying about.' He turned, opening his arms. She went up against him in the pewter starshine. Far away a great firework sped into the heavens and exploded, sending earthward a veritable cascade of multi-coloured little flickering stars.

CHAPTER SEVENTEEN

As Bonnie understood the following morning in her tiny office, the hardest of all things to do was concentrate upon one's work and close one's mind to one's heart, both at the same time.

Miss Singleton helped a good deal by appearing in Ward B, which was very unusual. But then she was on a very unusual mission.

'Mister Soguru, the gentleman from the Japanese consulate, telephoned earlier,

Bonnie, to ask if it would be all right if he brought round those Nipponese medics who are visiting the country. He'd like to make it before noon, if that would be all right with you.'

Bonnie said, 'With me? With *Doctor Fluornoy,* not I.'

The smooth Miss Singleton said, 'Doctor Fluornoy's already cleared it.' She paused briefly then said, 'And I told Mister Soguru it would be perfectly agreeable with you as well. A bit high-handed, wasn't I?'

Bonnie couldn't have felt annoyed if she'd wanted to. Miss Singleton was her friend. In fact, during that stormy meeting with the board of governors, she'd been just about Bonnie's only friend, at first.

There might have been time for a little visit between them except that Doctor Bryan telephoned to say he was having an amputee brought into Ward B from another ward. It was the young man who'd lost his left leg below the knee as a result of an auto accident. Bonnie didn't dissent; she had enough room, and moreover she also had the amputee's two recuperating friends who'd boned up on artificial limbs. She did, however, briefly wonder why Doctor Bryan had decided upon the change.

Perhaps, she speculated, because the amputee's friends were in Ward B, Bryan had decided to make the switch. Purposes of morale or something like that. She wasn't convinced Doctor Bryan was that wise, but, walking into the corridor with Miss Singleton she decided to give him full benefit of the doubt.

Miss Singleton, mistaking Bonnie's thoughtful mood to mean something else volunteered the information that the board members hadn't yet informed Doctor Fluornoy through her of whatever action they'd decided upon.

As before, this information did not move Bonnie one way or the other. She merely asked whether or not Doctor Fluornoy had appeared this morning. He had, said Miss Singleton; had closeted himself in his office and was writing again, as he'd spent the second half of the previous day.

About this siege of writing Miss Singleton was sanguinary. 'He's always detested doing it. When one of the medical societies have in past years asked him for papers on some surgical technique he's developed, he's either procrastinated until the deadline came and went, or else he's thrown together a hodge-podge and handed it to me with instructions to reorganize it and write it up. But this – whatever it is – that he's so engrossed in now...' Miss Singleton shrugged. She had no idea what it was. The last thing she said before taking the lift upstairs was: 'Take care; as soon as the visitors arrive I'll give you a warning buzz, then fetch them down.'

Bonnie returned to Ward B, found a note from Albert requesting that she meet him for tea at ten-thirty on her desk, and in response to a flicker of light on the Warning Board went up to the area where the newly arrived amputee was securely in place between his two friends.

The amputee was a curly-haired, fair and youthful man whose face still mirrored some of the trauma which had inevitably accompanied his drastic experience. But – and it was a definite tribute to John Fluornoy that he could do this – two days and one night after losing half a leg, he was able to smile at Bonnie, introduce himself, and ask if he mightn't have those two books his friends had told him of, the ones covering the subject of artificial limbs which his friends stoutly maintained were almost as efficient as natural limbs.

She said she'd have the books sent up,

checked his chart to see that it was properly current, and would have departed except that the young man also said, 'Miss Harper; I asked to be sent to your ward.'

Bonnie accepted that with a slow, tentative smile. She wasn't sure how the remark had been meant.

'All I've heard since coming round has been the pro and con talk about your revolutionary ideas. Anyway, I had a couple of friends here.'

Bonnie said, 'Hardly revolutionary, but certainly based upon *patient* morale rather than *staff* morale.' She would have gone then, it was getting close to the time to meet Albert in the cafeteria, but the youth spoke again.

'Miss Harper; my brother's a newspaperman. He's coming to visit me this afternoon. He called to ask if I was up to it. Of course I'm up to it. But I think except for that Doctor Fluornoy upstairs I wouldn't have been. Anyway, my brother said he'd be bringing along a photographer; he's heard about things out here too.'

She said she had to leave, that she'd have the books sent up straight away, and hastened down to the cafeteria, arriving there ten minutes late.

Albert was waiting, looking dreamily out of a window. He didn't seem aware of her tardiness as he arose, held her chair, signalled for a second cup of tea and smiled at her.

'Talked to your brother-in-law. The cottage is ours.'

She felt her heart turn over. 'Ours?'

'The price is considerably lower than I thought. I've already sent along a cheque. Your brother-in-law has agreed to handle the transaction.'

She ignored the tea when it arrived. 'Just like that, Albert?'

He snapped his fingers. 'Just like that we have a home. Own a home of our own. I sent word up to Doctor Fluornoy through his secretary we'd be checking out a bit early this afternoon. I even told her why.' He shoved his cup and saucer aside, lay a hand over her hand and leaned forward a little. 'I had no idea married – hmmm – soon-to-be-married man could be this happy, Bonnie. A wife, a home, love, beauty, softness – all within one week. I keep having those unnerving sensations it can't all be true.'

She didn't touch the tea. 'We'll make every bit of it come true. And more.' She didn't elaborate on what those last two words meant, instead she veered from the subject to mention the visiting Japanese doctors. He'd already heard of their coming. She also mentioned that Doctor Fluornoy was in his third floor office. He also knew that. He then asked if she'd heard anything respecting the board of governors. When she replied that she hadn't he gave her a little wry grin and said that adage about no news being good news didn't appear to be exactly correct.

'I don't like being kept in suspense. I suppose if they don't come up with something shortly it wouldn't be entirely out of order for me to contact them about acceptance of my resignation.'

She threw up her hands. There were too many important things all crowding up at once. 'Wait,' she implored. 'Let's have this foreign visitation finished with first, and give Doctor Fluornoy a chance to show his impatience before we do.' She smiled. 'I think he'll do that too.'

Albert was agreeable. In fact he acted as though she'd provided him with an excuse for backing off. 'I'll see you before three this afternoon,' he said. 'We'll duck out. Agreed?'

She nodded, radiant, and he might have

risked pecking her cheek except that she saw that look in his eye and sprang up murmuring something about having to hasten back.

She didn't recall the newsman and the photographer until, riding to the second floor on the lift alone, and then it was too late to tell him. Not that it was likely to matter much in any case.

Helen Cummings was in the office when Bonnie got back. She had a twinkle in her eye. 'There's incipient rebellion in Ward A,' she confided. 'Sampson is threatening to leave Nicholson if the new Ward Nurse carries out any innovations.' Before Bonnie could ask what had brought this about Cummings told her. 'Flowers on every bedstand this morning, and a new telly on a shelf at the lower end of the room.'

Bonnie mechanically smiled but she had a sinking feeling. From her previous discussion with Miss Sanderson she was willing to make a large wager Sanderson hadn't secured official permission for the changes.

At precisely eleven o'clock Mister Soguru and three bland Nipponese gentlemen arrived. Bonnie had a very hasty alert from Miss Singleton who neglected to mention that Doctor Fluornoy and two newspaper photographers were in the party, then she met the little cavalcade at the doorway. She'd previously alerted Helen Cummings, so everything was spick-and-span, the patients were ready, the room glistened, and Doctor Fluornoy's forbidding expression broke just once. That was when, after the formal introductions, he asked if she'd be kind enough to show them through, explaining the innovations, their theory and application, as they went. Then, with the others looking elsewhere, he dropped her a slow, solemn wink.

The Japanese gentlemen, fluent in English, stopped often to speak briefly with patients. The only time Bonnie failed to understand a word they said was when they paused beside the bed of the sailor. All talk here was in Japanese. Mister Soguru as well as the three eminent Nipponese medical practitioners crowded round this one bed, and while the sailor was obviously very impressed by the dazzling array of brilliant, successful men of his own race, he appeared to have no difficulty nor hesitation in conversing.

Bonnie stood back in the corridor with Doctor Fluornoy while this was going on. Old Fluornoy only once turned towards her. 'He's telling them Nicholson is the only hospital he's ever seen where the soul and spirit are treated equally with the body; that in his own case he is perfectly satisfied no such miraculous recovery would have been possible anywhere else in the world, including Nippon.'

Bonnie was too surprised at Doctor Fluornoy's knowledge of the Japanese language to comment. By the time she recovered from that Doctor Fluornoy was gravely stepping aside so the Nipponese could continue their walk up through Ward B.

Several times the news photographers fired blinding flash-bulbs. Once they got an excellent photo of Bonnie and Doctor Fluornoy standing side by side, apart from the visiting dignitaries.

Then it was over, Bonnie accompanied them out into the large corridor and faintly flushed as Mister Soguru made a very flowery speech, smiling at her all the while. All the Japanese bowed and she, uncertain, bowed back. Doctor Fluornoy, a little stiffer in either the spine or the spirit, only bobbed his head. Then, turning as Bonnie was about to return to her ward, he said, 'I'd like to see you right after luncheon in my office, Miss Harper,' and stalked away with the Japanese gentlemen leaving her to speculate.

Back in the tiny office she dropped into the desk-chair feeling the let-down. The telephone buzzed. It was Miss Singleton asking whether or not Doctor Fluornoy was available. Bonnie said he wasn't, but that Miss Singleton might catch him on the mezzanine where he'd gone, accompanying the visiting Japanese to their car.

She'd scarcely hung up when Mister McCann's buzzer flashed on the lighted panel in front of her desk. She didn't really feel up to a session with Mister McCann, just yet, but since none of her subordinate nurses were handy she pushed herself out of the chair and went along.

McCann wasn't his usual blustery self. He was in fact surprisingly mild, almost sly, and he asked how the inspection had gone off. She thought it had been successful. He agreed with that. Then he asked if the board of governors had called her since their visit two days previous. They hadn't, she informed him, but they may have seen Doctor Fluornoy because she was to go to his office right after luncheon. McCann showed her that almost villainous little hard smile of his and said, 'Well, don't let me keep you, Miss Harper. It's lunch time right now.'

She wasn't satisfied at all with the

interview but on the other hand she was both anxious to meet Albert in the cafeteria – if he happened to be there when she arrived – and she also had a feeling that if she'd asked what, specifically, McCann's interest was, he wouldn't have told her.

She found Helen Cummings in the office, said she'd be in the cafeteria if wanted, and left the ward. Outside, Doctor Bryan was just emerging from Ward A. She stiffened instinctively but he only smiled, nodded briskly and walked off. She assumed the engagement ring had done its work and slowly crossed to the lift.

The day was only half spent and she felt as though she'd already been fifteen hours on a treadmill. But she was perfectly satisfied about one point: the Japanese delegation had been favourably impressed with Ward B.

CHAPTER EIGHTEEN

Albert wasn't in the cafeteria, which was buzzing with talk of the Japanese visitation, among other things, and Miss Sanderson of Ward A came over to lay a large hand lightly upon Bonnie's shoulder, squeeze, then walk off without a word. No word had been necessary anyway.

Lunch helped but on the way to the third floor afterwards Bonnie had the feeling that her triumphs and defeats were somehow intermingled. She tried to separate them and failed, although she did not quite feel that her failings were noticeable outwardly; where she felt she'd most particularly failed was where Doctor Fluornoy was concerned. She tried to analyse his expression and attitude during the visit of the Japanese delegation.

It was difficult because of that craggily forbidding look of his. Even his slightly aloof, grave bearing hadn't been entirely convincing either way. She gave it up as the lift halted and she stepped forth into the quiet, sedate third-floor corridor.

Miss Singleton was at her desk when Bonnie entered. She pushed a button twice on her desk and arose to say Doctor Fluornoy was waiting. She even opened the door for Bonnie.

The window was open letting in both sunlight and fresh air. John Fluornoy was at his desk amid a clutter of paper. He neither smiled nor scowled as he arose and motioned Bonnie to the chair opposite the desk. As she sat, though, he said, 'Well; I shouldn't be too surprised if you received the Order of the Rising Sun. Our Japanese doctors were very impressed.' He looked soberly at her. 'At least they *acted* as though they were, although I can tell you from some experience among Japanese that it's difficult at any time to correctly assess their moods – and motives.'

He sat down, looked at his hands a moment, then raised those glacial pale eyes once again. 'The newspapers now have something to write about too. One of those photographers was a local man. The other was hired by the Japanese consulate. Public relations for the doctors back home.'

Bonnie got the impression that Doctor Fluornoy was talking all around whatever it was that had occasioned his request that she come to his office, so she sat politely attentive and silent. She was right, too. After a bit he asked about the wedding plans, his objective apparently being to get her into the conversation. She told him about the house, about leaving a bit early with Albert to select furnishings, then she waited again while he scanned one of the sheets of paper before him.

Ultimately he said, 'Of course I'm delighted for both of you,' and cleared his throat as though ready to plunge into something altogether different. 'I have been informed that the board of governors would like to meet with you, Doctor Heath, and me, tomorrow morning. I'll see that you're notified when the board arrives.' He smoothed out a perfectly smooth piece of paper on the desk. In a very different tone he then said, 'There is one thing I loathe above most other things: writing. Writing reports, letters, technical papers. But this mess on the desk is the one exception ... I suppose I did it as much to clear up some fuzzy thoughts of my own as to make public Nicholson's stand on change within the institution. It's helped me understand a lot of things I just did not have time for before.' He looked straight at her. 'But – I'm not much of a writer, and although Althea Singleton usually does these things for me, in this case what I think we need is someone who *feels* what I've tried to impartially say in these pages. In short, Miss Harper, I called you up here today to hand you this unpleasant task.' He scooped up the papers very suddenly, as though he might have been building up to this moment deliberately, held them out across the desk and said, 'Take it all home with you. Read it, touch it up, explain where I've been unable to quite catch the mood, and give it back to me first thing in the morning. I want copies made to present to the governors when they arrive.'

She accepted the loose pieces of paper with a rising feeling of near-panic. She'd been a very poor essayist in school, and like Doctor Fluornoy, had put off writing letters as much as possible. Now, confronted with a task she knew was entirely beyond her abilities, she sat looking helplessly at his cramped handwriting feeling very inadequate. When the shock abated and she looked up, he didn't give her a chance to protest, but, leaning upon the desk looking grim as death, he drove home the points of his contention.

'The first significant changes in hospital procedures have been inaugurated here at Nicholson in order to synthesize treatment with the catalyst being equally shared by medicine and post-operative and post-illness therapy.'

He paused. She knew he was speaking from memory from his writings, and while she understood both words and meaning, all his statement did was confirm her sense of inadequacy. He seemed to sense this for when next he spoke, relaxing, leaning back in his chair, he smiled.

'Well; something like that anyway. And I don't want you to delete your name any time you see it in those pages. What all this boils down to is that you have started a revolution in hospital care, and while I've dragged my feet ... after all I'm at an age where one just naturally resists change ... since listening to those ignoramuses in here the other day – Staunton, Belcher and Funston – I've come to what is commonly referred to as an Agonizing Reappraisal. In blunt terms I was wrong, admit that, and now wish to give full support to your ideas.' He threw up his hands. 'That's all.'

At last he gave her an opportunity to speak, but wisely, he'd kept her from it long enough for the full impact to soak in. In other words, sitting there gazing over at him, she knew that whatever she said was going to sound very inane. She was also very aware that he'd think so too.

She simply said, 'I'll do my best but I should warn you, I'm not a writer by the wildest stretch of the imagination.'

'Enthusiasm,' he said, 'is what the report

needs. Enthusiasm and feeling. You'll have both because what I've said in those pages was based entirely on your own feelings.'

He stood up, his way of indicating the interview was over. But he smiled again. 'Perhaps Doctor Heath may be of some help. And Althea Singleton. Call on anyone you need – me included, but just don't fail me. I'll need that report to hand to the board members in the morning.'

He crossed over, opened the door for her, and as she mechanically passed forth into his outer office he said, 'This will find its way into the newspapers, eventually, I presume, so please state our case in as convincing a manner as possible – Bonnie.'

She wasn't even conscious of his use of her first name until he'd closed the door at her back. When she eventually *did* recall it though, she also recalled never having heard him use anyone's first name before.

Miss Singleton was helpful. When Bonnie explained, she offered to meet after hours with Bonnie and Albert Heath and con-tribute whatever talent she possessed to whipping the report into shape. Bonnie gave her Beth's home address, thanked her and went back down to Ward B, quite unaware that it was by then almost three o'clock.

What reminded her was a note Miss Cummings handed her the moment she stepped into the tiny office. It was from Albert; he'd be waiting in the car downstairs.

She changed, rolled the sheaf of loose papers into a little round bundle, stuffed them into her purse and left Ward B without a word to Miss Cummings, who watched her departure with great interest as well as great curiosity. Miss Cummings had never before seen Miss Harper so entirely at a loss.

Albert was waiting. He held the door for her and as they drove away she told him of her dilemma. He accepted it with grave interest and shed the only ray of light anyone had thus far shed. He said he'd been very successful in college as a debater and essayist.

She was relieved and slowly lost her feeling of helplessness and inadequacy. But he also told her he would only *help* with the drafting, that he agreed with Doctor Fluornoy; since the entire thing had been her idea, she should do the writing.

Albert was not in the least perturbed, and that added to her confidence too, so that by the time they got into the heart of the city where the furniture stores were, she was recovering fast from the shock of her new and weighty assignment.

They looked at furniture until after five o'clock. By then most of the stores were closing anyway. They'd selected about one-third of all they needed and over another of those early suppers at his favourite restaurant, compared ideas, notes, and plans for their cottage.

By the time he was ready to take her home – she vetoed his suggestion that they go to a theatre because of the awesome chore lying ahead of her – she was almost eager to get to the rewriting.

The really professional help that eventually materialized came from an unthought-of source. Charles listened to Bonnie's report of the thing she had to do, took the pages and quietly studied them as he relaxed as was his custom on the verandah. Then he said almost casually, 'There's not much to this.'

Bonnie and Albert exchanged a look, a dawning hope between them. She said, 'Charles; could you help us – perhaps suggest a proper format, some sound, concise arguments?'

He winked at his wife. 'For a fee,' he said.

'In fact for a decent fee I'll do the whole job for you.'

'We couldn't impose...' Bonnie murmured, but with a flooding light of prodigious relief filling her eyes which scarcely fit her words.

Charles laughed and turned to his wife. 'How long before dinner?'

'Half an hour, love.'

He arose, taking the loose pages in one big hand. 'Be busy for the next half hour,' he said, and went into the house.

Bonnie slumped and Beth chuckled. 'Were you dreading it all that much?'

'Worse,' she said, and, remembering Miss Singleton's offer to come round, got out of her chair. 'I've got to make a telephone call and tell someone they needn't rush over tonight.'

As Bonnie disappeared into the house, Albert smiled at Beth. 'You have a very remarkable husband,' he said.

Beth didn't dispute that, she only said, 'I also have a very remarkable sister, Doctor Heath.'

They talked a bit about the cottage. Beth was pleased it had all worked out so well. She listened as Albert told of the delegation of visiting Japanese. She used that serene, wise little smile of hers as she murmured pleasure on that score also. Then she asked about their wedding plans.

They hadn't made any. In fact, the more Albert thought about it the more it seemed they might have to postpone the wedding. 'Just too many things happening that will take time.'

'Was it Bonnie's idea, getting wed next Friday?'

Albert said it was. He would have given a broader explanation but Beth didn't allow him to.

She said, 'Doctor; might a meddling sister-in-law make a diagnosis? If she has her mind set on a Friday wedding, go right along with it. That is, of course, if you really want to.'

He made a short exclamation. 'Want to, Mrs Hamilton? I've never wanted anything so much in my life. But it occurred to me she'd want something planned, a little elaborate perhaps – something memorable.'

Beth's smile turned into a rich, soft chuckle. 'Believe me, Doctor, a woman's wedding is memorable even if it's held in a small country church. No matter where or how it's accomplished, it is forever after remembered through a particularly private and golden aura.'

He accepted that because it obviously was quite true. If he'd never thought of weddings in that light it only proved he was ignorant of the mechanics of marriage. But he would find out a lot of things before another week had passed.

Bonnie returned to say she'd caught Miss Singleton as she'd been preparing to leave her apartment, had explained how their dilemma had been resolved, and Miss Singleton had been delighted for them all.

Bonnie also confided to Beth and Albert that as she'd passed down the hallway past Charles's study she'd heard his typewriter hammering away at a great rate. She'd had no idea he could type, as well as compose things for typing.

Beth said, 'My dear, there's an awful lot you don't know about my Charles. He has a side to him I don't suppose – excepting me – anyone really knows.'

Neither Bonnie nor Albert would, or could, have disputed that, and at this particular moment neither wanted to dispute it.

CHAPTER NINETEEN

Beth insisted Albert stay for dinner. He didn't really need much coaxing but he did explain he and Bonnie'd had a meal only an hour or two earlier. Later, when Charles came to the verandah, both girls were in the kitchen. Charles handed Albert the finished pages stapled together and also threw him a quizzical look.

'This Doctor Fluornoy – if he talks like he writes, no one would be able to ever prove whether he was a genius or a charlatan. What's the point of using medical terms in a paper you're slanting for non-medical people?'

Albert didn't know, but then he'd never read Doctor Fluornoy's article – or whatever it was – either. He simply said, 'Well, you see the idea was that Bonnie would be able to breathe *life* into the article while John Fluornoy did the reasoning and–'

'Right enough,' conceded Charles. 'I tried to keep that in mind when I toned the thing down.'

Albert's misgivings sounded in his voice. 'Toned it down, Mister Hamilton...?'

'Made it more plebeian, Doctor Heath; more human and less lofty. In other words, I rewrote it as I imagine Bonnie would have thought and written.'

Albert still appeared dubious but Charles, surveying the younger man's expression, smiled and arose. 'Read it,' he said. 'I'll go mix us a couple of Bloody Marys.'

Bonnie came to the front door to tell Albert he might wash if he wished, saw him reading and walked on out. Albert looked up at her. It was a little difficult reading the entire article without sufficient light but he didn't have to read all of it anyway.

'Extraordinary,' he told her. 'I'd just never have thought him capable of this.' He handed it to her but she simply held it making no effort to read it.

'That's good, Albert?'

'The man's done precisely what Doctor Fluornoy had in mind; he's made the thing seem as though you were speaking. Except for the sharply clear masculine logic, this whole thing could be you, love.'

She sat, held the papers in both hands and said, 'Beth used to say Charles could have been just as gifted a writer or actor as an attorney. I thought she was biased; he just has never struck me as very creative. Albert; I'm so glad *someone* had the gift. I knew that even with your help, I'd never have been able to do it the way Doctor Fluornoy expected me to.' She arose. 'Come along; Beth sent me out to tell you to wash up, dinner's ready.'

When he arose looking somewhat sceptical about that also, she smiled and took his hand. 'You don't really have to gorge you know. I'm just as unhungry as you are.'

Charles met them at the door with two highballs. He handed one to Albert and raised his eyebrows at Bonnie. She shook her head, warmly thanked him for what he'd done with John Fluornoy's article, then said she'd go help Beth, for them to come along when they'd finished their drinks.

Charles passed on outside. He listened to Albert's expressions of gratitude gazing far off into the soft night, then he sipped and said, 'Doctor; in a sense you and I are both overly educated.'

Albert looked round sharply.

'What I mean is that while I was rewriting that paper it once more occurred to me that when people are continually educated throughout all their formative years, right up until they're no longer even remotely young, they've layers upon layers of second-hand knowledge laid over their instincts until, *cum laude,* they are little old people without ever having been young at all.' Charles's sardonic, steady gaze settled upon Albert. 'This Doctor Fluornoy ... the more I read that paper the sorrier I felt for him. He is an old man who never had a chance to be young. He expounds ideas in his paper that are wistful, beseeching, searching. Fresh ideals, he says, and youthful horizons are what are needed in the field of post-operative care. A synthesis of old knowledge with fresh, wholesome idealism. Doctor Heath – that whole paper is an old man's cry in the night for a youth he never really had; he wants others to see that youth is given its creative chance.'

Albert, who hadn't read very much of the paper, finished his highball and considered the cool glass in his hand. Charles Hamilton was truly an extraordinary person. There was a depth to him one simply would not have suspected at all. Albert wondered how many dozens of people had known Charles – and still knew him – who had never even glimpsed what depths were below the surface of the man.

Bonnie appeared in the doorway. 'Dinner,' she said. 'Have you two finished your drinks?'

They had so they went indoors.

Beth was addicted to intimate little dinners by candlelight. Her reasons were romantic, which she frankly admitted, but she also nodded towards the huge dining-room window beyond which shone the steady kaleidoscope of city lights below and far away. Obviously, with the dining-room lights on that breathtaking view would have been sharply minimized.

Bonnie and Albert, not particularly hungry, went through the motions of eating and kept a lively conversation going. Charles seemed to be enjoying himself. As he eventually said, nothing, not excluding the finest wines, settled a good dinner quite so well, nor complemented it so thoroughly, as good conversation.

Afterwards, while Beth and Bonnie cleaned up, the men returned again to the warm shadows of the verandah. Charles said he'd set up the mechanical routine which would secure the cottage for Albert and Bonnie. He also said that although he'd never seen that particular house, he'd known the artist who'd built and lived in it, and he wasn't surprised to hear it described in superlatives.

Albert, leaning back in his chair as solidly content as a man might be, listened as Charles talked. Actually, neither of them were loquacious men, and yet, together, they managed quite easily to keep an interesting conversation going. It seemed they shared a quiet thoughtfulness based upon a mutual sense of decent values. Albert reflected upon this and was pleased; obviously Beth was Bonnie's favourite person. It would help greatly if the four of them got on well.

Later, when the women joined them, Bonnie said she wanted to show Albert the garden and took him out there. He of course made no mention of having seen the garden before. If Bonnie wished to be alone with him that was perfectly agreeable with him.

He thanked Beth for the supper, for the highball and the hospitality. Beth smiled. Charles and Albert exchanged a look. Charles made a droll face and slowly raised and lowered one eyelid. They were men – healthy men. They understood one another perfectly.

Watching her sister and Doctor Heath stroll away Beth said, 'Charles; how good is the article?'

'Good enough, love,' he said almost indifferently. 'Doctor Fluornoy, whose reputation is very well established, is simply asking for indulgence and justifying his request in medical terms. I kicked out a good deal of his tongue-twisters and substituted common names. He doesn't intend for the paper to sway a community of other medics, and he most certainly knows, since he has written so little and is so well known, that it will get into the newspapers, therefore it should be understandable to the average chap.

'Also; he seems to be justifying the innovations your sister has instituted at Nicholson. In that he's quite convincing. But then I may be biased; I always was weak where a good figure was concerned.'

'Charles!'

He smiled at her. 'Don't worry. Even if the hospital governing board is hidebound it'll have to step very carefully once this thing reaches the newspapers. People will invariably side with someone who sympathizes with people rather than with ruling bodies. It's human nature; we're all more or less in awe of the professions, love; we respect, admire, and deeply envy at the same time.'

'Isn't that psychology, Charles?'

'What isn't?' he asked. 'A pleasant supper by candlelight, a highball before dinner, an old man's efforts at convincing others as well as himself that change is right as well as inevitable – those things are all psychological.' Charles turned, a roguish twinkle in his eye. 'Even taking a young man down into the garden by starlight.'

Beth was momentarily silent. They couldn't see nor hear Bonnie and Albert. Music came distantly from inside the house where the wireless set was serenading them. It was pleasant on the verandah. Eventually she said, thinking ahead, 'The best thing that ever happened to Bonnie was coming here. I've worried a lot the last two or three years. Young girls are so impressionable.'

He didn't seem to have heard. He was sitting with his head upon the back of his chair, eyes closed.

'And this has worked out splendidly. Doctor Heath is an answer to a prayer.

He still sat loose and easy, eyes closed, body slumped. But this time he spoke. 'They've got a nice little mess ahead of them, love. There always has been and

216

always will be, resistance to change. It may all appear romantic and roseate here and now, but don't let starlight and nighttime fragrance delude you. I've a feeling that before their little tempest is over they'll wish several times it had never come at all.'

'But it will end right, won't it, Charles?'

He was just as casual about that too. 'It will end right, of course. Most things do. It's somewhere between the beginning of a scrap and the end that people are shaken down enough to see themselves as well as their enemies in the light of pure reality.'

He yawned. It hadn't been a particularly hard day for him but it *had* been a long one. Nonetheless he made no move to go indoors.

Beth sat with the inward serenity not many women possess, looking out where darkness had made its imprint, thoughts quietly forming, breaking up and reforming, each time presenting the patterns of alternatives which are the unknown future.

The fact that she knew her husband better than anyone else did, understood his capacity for correct prognostication, helped to allay any fears she might otherwise have had. But primarily Beth was satisfied;

whether a battle came out of Bonnie's creativity at Nicholson or not, Beth was convinced of one thing: Bonnie had found exactly the ingredients for personal happiness. No woman could expect more. In fact, not many women even came close to finding these ingredients. Many thought they had, but in every newspaper across the face of the earth divorce notices proved conclusively that this was not so.

Eventually Charles said unless he retired now he'd fall asleep in the chair, so she went inside with him, leaving the little verandah-light lit for her sister, and also, when Charles wasn't looking, she stepped to the railing and cast a searching glance down into the garden. It was quite dark down there, and shadowy, but she was certain they were sitting close upon the little bench.

The reason she heard nothing was because for a long while they simply sat, saying nothing, or saying very little in low tones. It was, as Albert said, the night of the crisis. They'd be told next morning when the governing board met in Doctor Fluornoy's office whether they'd still be required at Nicholson or not. He also told her he thought the board might have been religiously searching for replacements.

'Not entirely because they're dissatisfied with us, but because *our* decisions are just as important to them as their decisions are to us. They'd be foolish to risk losing three key staff members without taking some steps to have replacements handy if that's what it comes to.'

She hadn't been able to work up a lot of enthusiasm – or anxiety – since the day of the last meeting. She'd adopted the philosophy that she was finished at Nicholson in any event, and moreover, something else had intervened; something that would in any case have taken her mind off whatever other dedications she might have had: marriage.

No woman can think of impending marriage, and other things, simultaneously. Marriage filled her mind, her imagination, even her dreams. She told him that and kissed his cheek.

But he was a man, which meant he was quite capable of dwelling upon other things; it was natural for as a provider he couldn't lose sight of all else. He didn't say that. It's doubtful if he even recognized it in himself, nevertheless he turned at her touch, took her in his arms and for a little while forgot the other things.

She said, 'I feel sorry for Doctor Fluornoy.'

He didn't answer, instead he sought her full lips. They locked together in a tender-fierce embrace until, over at the house, they heard a door quietly close, then he loosened, gazed at his wristwatch, looked again because it just didn't seem possible it could be so late, then arose, pulling her up with him.

'Time I went home,' he said, and at her look of disappointment he bent close and whispered: 'After next Friday you may wish I *would* go home.'

She smiled into his eyes. 'After next Friday, love, you *will* be home – every night, all night.'

CHAPTER TWENTY

The sense of crisis reached her the following morning as she sat in Ward B's office reading the charts and reports left by the Night Ward Nurse. She could feel her nerves knotting, could feel the steel band round her heart. It was a delayed reaction –

very delayed in fact – and when Miss Singleton's soothing voice came down the telephone to her she loosened a little expecting to be told the board was convening upstairs and that her presence was required. Instead, Miss Singleton said there were two men waiting in Doctor Fluornoy's office to see her. One was a news photographer, the other was a reporter.

Evidently both men were within hearing-distance of Miss Singleton's desk, for the veiled warning Miss Singleton offered next was very softly said. 'Doctor has given the gentlemen his statement. He asks that you show them round – and refer any technical questions back to him.' After a little pause during which Bonnie thought she caught the innuendo, Miss Singleton also said, 'If I send a girl down for the report will it be ready; Doctor Fluornoy would like to see it before the meeting this morning.'

Bonnie said she'd have it ready and rang off, arose and walked out of the office. Being an active, healthy person nervousness always prompted physical release. She went up through the ward, stopped wherever she was called, and went over to look at the title of the book the amputee was holding. It was one on artificial limbs. The young man was almost cheerful. He said, 'I had no idea these things were this refined.'

Her answer was practical. 'No one is until they have to be. I imagine you've talked to a dozen people in your lifetime who've had artificial legs without ever knowing it.'

The Japanese seaman was sitting up. He widely smiled as she held out one of the little sticks of incense from a pocket. 'I think the others are learning to like the smell,' she said.

Mister McCann was also propped up. He told her he was feeling so much better he was going to ask to be released. She said she'd send Doctor Heath over as soon as she could.

McCann cocked a shrewd, tough eye. 'Isn't it this morning you're to go before the inquisitors?'

She wondered how he knew and asked. 'Yes; I'm expecting the call momentarily. But it's not general knowledge, Mister McCann. You must have a very efficient spy upstairs.'

He chuckled. 'Not upstairs, lassie, *downstairs* and in the municipal buildings.' He turned serious. 'What the devil would board members who've never been in this place know about how it should be operated?'

She used the stock hospital answer to that question. 'I scarcely think someone needs to spend six months in the city jail, Mister McCann, to know how it should be operated.'

Rebuked, he squinted at her. 'Whose side are you on – your own side or *their* side?'

She showed him that sweet smile and said, 'The side of the hospital,' and went on up the ward where Albert had just appeared through the far doorway.

Albert reported seeing the board members arrive only a short while before. He doubted that they'd have time to get much of a hearing under way for another half hour. Someone was detaining them downstairs just outside the main doorways. Albert thought it might have been newsmen. She asked if he'd go look at Mister McCann, squeezed his arm and went along to visit her other patients.

She was speaking to Helen Cummings about an elderly man's medication when a very young girl in a uniform of a nurse's aide came up asking for some papers to be taken to Miss Singleton in Doctor Fluornoy's office. Bonnie went back to the ward office, handed them over and was about to step into the corridor when two men came in, one carrying a camera. This man had a folded newspaper pushed into a jacket pocket. He smiled, but as it turned out he had practically nothing at all to say. It was his companion, a youngish, quick, Lincolnesque man named Dabney who was the reporter. Dabney also asked the questions and made the observations.

In an almost reproachful manner he took the folded paper from his companion, spread it out for Bonnie to see, and pointed to a brace of pictures upon the front page. One showed Bonnie and Doctor Fluornoy side by side, the other showed Mister Soguru and the delegation of visiting Japanese medical men.

'And that,' said Dabney, 'was a stab in the back, Miss. My paper should've had that layout, not this rag.'

Bonnie felt neither sympathetic nor rebuked. She said, 'I'm a little pressed for time, gentlemen, so if you'd like some pictures and some questions answered perhaps we'd better get on with it.'

Dabney looked sharply at her, apparently saw her resolution and toughness, something very few men ever saw in a beautiful girl, and became brisk again.

She held them at the lower end of the

ward for nearly ten minutes explaining things; the colour scheme on the walls and ceiling, the flowers, newspapers, the deliberate candour she'd schooled her nurses in. The atmosphere of relaxed friendship among patients and the attitude of good-natured comradeship between patients and ward staff.

When Dabney asked a question she'd shot an answer straight back. His companion took at least a dozen pictures and while the patients were aware of what was in progress only one raised up to beckon for the photographer to get closer – get very close, in fact, and get the patient's broadly smiling face into proper focus.

McCann.

Albert came through from across the corridor, was introduced to Bonnie's visitors and agreed to pose with her. He was wearing a raffish little smile when the photograph was taken. *She* knew and *he* knew that if Mister Dabney'd had an inkling they were in love, were engaged, he'd also put that into his article. Neither told him.

Finally, Dabney asked if it would be permissible for him to go interview some of the patients. Bonnie thought it might be a good idea. So did Doctor Heath. As soon as

Dabney and his ectoplasmic photographer walked off Albert jerked his head towards the little office and led the way.

'I called upstairs a bit ago,' he told her when they had privacy. 'Miss Singleton said the board members walked in not a minute earlier. She said Doctor Fluornoy had just finished reading the rewritten report and had sent it back for her to have copied and brought back to him. She is to make ten copies on the duplicating machine as fast as she can.'

'Ten copies?'

Albert said, 'Three for the board, one for him, one for you, me, and I presume one to files. The balance to the press. I'm only guessing. Anyway, the point I'm making is that he's pleased with the rewriting.'

'Bully for him,' she said softly, unaware until she'd said it just how cynical it sounded. Then she said, 'I'm sorry. I didn't mean it as it sounded; I suppose the waiting is making me edgy.'

He stooped a little, brushed his lips across her mouth and straightened back. He just barely got away with it; Mister Dabney and the photographer squeezed into the office to thank her for all her help. They shook hands with Doctor Heath also. Dabney, with a roguish look, said, 'Watch the evening paper, Miss Harper. I think we've got something here. Something controversial. We've covered a lot of hospitals – including this one – over the years, and never have we come up with anything revolutionary in any of 'em until today. That's what makes good copy.'

Dabney paused to consider his notes then stuffed them into his pocket. He pursed his lips the way a man might who'd be arriving at some careful assessment. He looked round as though someone might be eavesdropping then said, 'McCann; do you know who he is?'

Bonnie and Albert both nodded. They knew. She particularly knew because Mister McCann had never been willing to hide his light under a bushel.

'Didn't know *he* was in here.'

Albert asked what McCann had said, Dabney's pursed lips drooped. He said Mister McCann had praised Nicholson, but he'd said Ward B was a model of what every hospital ward should be. 'He also said Miss Harper is a genius in her vocation.' Dabney's dull eyes brightened a little. 'None of it can hurt you,' he told Bonnie. What Dabney *didn't* say was that McCann had been very emphatic about one thing: he was of the opinion that every major hospital should have one administrative head ward nurse whose duties would include complete supervision of hospital morale, procedures, routines, and wards. That came out later in the papers, but by the time Bonnie and Albert Heath saw it, steps had already been taken to implement it.

After the newsmen departed the mail arrived. Albert was called over to Ward A so Bonnie opened one bulky letter addressed to her personally, quite alone in the office. The Japanese consulate had sent her a very handsome parchment designed for framing, but the only part she could read was her name – hand-engraved in Old English. She took the thing up to the seaman to have it interpreted.

He read it over very carefully, then, wearing a broad smile, told her the plaque was a commendation for her 'devotion to duty, her selfless dedication to the ill people in her care, and offered her the great honour of Honoured Citizen of Nippon'.

She was embarrassed and delighted. Embarrassed because she thought the award should have mentioned Nicholson and her ward staff, delighted because this was the first recognition of her innovations to come along. She promised to have it framed and hung conspicuously on the wall, and returned to the office to finish reading the mail.

There was another letter, much less flowery, much more crisp. It was an offer from another hospital. The pay was much better and she'd have full charge of social and non-technical administration. That letter she carefully folded and tucked into a pocket.

Miss Cummings came along to say the mail had been distributed, the patients were taken care of, and she'd like to go down to the cafeteria for her mid-morning cup of tea.

Bonnie sent her along.

For a short while now, as always this time of day, the rush stopped. There were no fresh admittees, the other nurses were able to relax for a while, and Bonnie ordinarily would also have paid a visit to the cafeteria. This morning she did not. The Japanese plaque lay before her on the little desk, the heartening offer of an administrative position was in her pocket. She actually felt a lot better than she'd felt before, while she awaited the fateful call from upstairs.

Albert returned to say Elvira Sampson had left Nicholson. Bonnie was surprised. 'But she can't possibly have recovered that fast.'

He was tart. 'No. But she could hobble, and she flatly refused to stay in a hospital which was being turned into a social club with curtains, incense, newspapers and television sets.'

'You cleared her, Albert?'

'With great pleasure. I even went down in the lift with her and saw her into a taxi.' He smiled. 'You might even say I pushed a little as she was climbing into the auto.'

Thinking of Elvira Sampson and Miss Sanderson, Ward Nurse across the hallway, Bonnie decided they were just too much alike in one respect; both were tough, fearless, outspoken. Sanderson wouldn't have taken a thing off Sampson.

Albert broke across her thoughts saying, 'Forget it, love. There will always be Elvira Sampsons. If you brood about one you'll brood about them all, and they just aren't worth the time.'

The telephone rang. She and Albert gazed at it, neither of them with the slightest doubt that this was the summons to whatever course their personal futures would take.

He reached first, spoke his name, listened a bit then replaced the instrument upon its cradle. 'Miss Singleton,' he said, and did not elaborate. 'Do you need a cup of coffee or something?'

She handed him the Japanese plaque first, then showed him the letter from the other hospital. She didn't need any bolstering at all, she said, beyond those two things. He agreed, and still holding the Japanese award led the way out of the office, across the room out into the yonder corridor. There, waiting beside the lift, he grinned almost impishly.

'I'm looking forward to this.'

She wasn't. At least, while she was a lot more assured than she had been up until an hour ago, she did not look forward to the unpleasant aspects of what lay ahead.

He gave her arm a little squeeze as they stepped into the lift, and as the doors slid closed soundlessly and they were hidden, he turned her, swayed her against him and kissed her.

CHAPTER TWENTY-ONE

Miss Singleton was waiting, looking harassed for the first time since Bonnie had known her. She pointed to the little stacks of pages. 'The report,' she said, and grimaced. 'I'm going to ask that Nicholson acquire an electric duplicating machine. That hand-crank almost gave me blisters.'

Albert gravely took her right hand, looked closely and said, raising his eyes, 'I see nothing here but the strong, willing hand of a very lovely woman.'

Miss Singleton smiled at him and winked at Bonnie. 'I'd watch this one if I were you, Miss Harper.' Then the little magic moment passed and she said, 'I'll bring these things in as soon as I've stapled them together. Meanwhile – all I can tell you is that Staunton, Belcher and Funston have been in there with Doctor Fluornoy for about fifteen minutes and since I've heard no profanity nor howls of indignation, they must be having a more or less amicable meeting.' She motioned towards the closed door. 'I'm to send you both in the moment you arrive. Good luck.'

Albert opened the door, stepped aside for Bonnie to enter first, then followed after, closing the door very gently. The men all rose and smiled. Doctor Fluornoy's smile was slightly forced as he said, 'Good morning, Miss Harper – Doctor Heath – there are chairs.' He dropped down behind the desk as soon as he'd dispensed with the amenities and considered his hands atop the desk. Evidently whatever he and the board members had been discussing up to now wasn't relevant to what would now ensue.

That same little awkward silence followed which had occurred previously when they'd all met, only this time it was Bonnie who broke it. Looking past at John Fluornoy she relayed what Miss Singleton had said; the copies of the report would be along soon.

Doctor Fluornoy smiled acknowledgement then gazed at the three men arranged in front of his desk and said, 'I've already explained about the article, gentlemen, so until each of you have a copy perhaps we'd best move on to – other things.'

Bonnie saw Albert straighten perceptibly in his chair. She felt the tension too.

Mister Belcher turned to Bonnie. He'd

seen the article in the newspapers about the Japanese delegation. He thought she should be commended for the excellent impression she'd made.

As though on cue Albert held forth the award for the board members to see. They studied it soberly and Staunton, looking not the least abashed suggested someone have the thing interpreted into English. Bonnie gave the version the sailor had given her. Staunton was appeased, as were Belcher and Funston.

Then Mister Funston said the board had held several Executive Sessions since the lot of them had last met in Doctor Fluornoy's office. He was vague, though, saying simply, 'Hospital policy must be cleared through the governing board. *Must* be, otherwise I needn't point out that some variety of chaos will follow. But I don't want to leave the impression the board is hard-headed nor unsympathetic. It isn't – not at all.'

Mister Staunton seemed a little less than enchanted by all this so as soon as Funston paused, searching for additional words, Staunton said, 'Doctor Heath and Miss Harper; we voted not to accept those resignations. We also voted against accepting Doctor Fluornoy's resignation. That's what we've been discussing until you folks got here. Of course all that means is that the Board doesn't want any of you to resign; it doesn't mean we could possibly keep any of you against your will. But,' Staunton fished among his outside pockets, then his inside pockets, and eventually brought forth a pair of typewritten pages which he used to gesture with, 'but; since there's a move abroad to cut Nicholson's budget for the coming fiscal year we should tell you right now that if this thing goes through there'll be no chance for increases in salary for anyone.'

'And that,' said John Fluornoy stonily, 'means, gentlemen, you'll never be able to keep any of the present staff at Nicholson.'

Staunton lowered the papers to his lap, fixed old Fluornoy with a level look and said, 'For your information, Doctor, this damned thing is signed by a Chairman of the Allocations Board – Fred McCann.'

Bonnie's heart skipped a beat but she was the only one in the room who seemed surprised. Perhaps she shouldn't have been since she now remembered who Mister McCann officially was. She just hadn't had time to think about that lately.

John Fluornoy was smiling at Staunton. 'I

can assure you, Ed, I had nothing whatsoever to do with that. I've only seen McCann a time or two since he's been here.'

Staunton and the others turned next to consider Bonnie and Albert, but neither of them looked guilty because neither of them were.

Funston, reaching to take the papers from Staunton, said, 'Where'd you get this, Ed?'

'In my morning mail. And I also got something else. Miss Singleton's resignation.'

Belcher didn't like that. 'She'd be hard to replace. How long's she been here, Doctor Fluornoy?'

'Ten or eleven years. As long as I have.'

Staunton brushed this aside. 'One more thing, ladies and gentlemen: since the article on the visiting Japanese dignitaries came out, my office has been besieged by calls from other hospitals for permission to send people to Nicholson to study our new methods.' Staunton shook his head. 'I was purposefully vague about all this.'

Albert said, 'There will be more, Mister Staunton. Perhaps Doctor Fluornoy has told you, but this morning a team from the city's largest newspaper came round to take photos and hold interviews. Miss Harper and I were informed the entire series would begin in this evening's papers.'

Staunton looked sharply at old Fluornoy and got back an unperturbed gaze. Fluornoy said, 'Nothing to feel piqued about, Ed. I'd have told you when we got round to it.'

Belcher was visibly shaken. He turned to Funston and Staunton. 'We're being led down the path.' The others were uncomfortable but not that rattled. Funston merely shrugged.

Bonnie chose this moment to take the letter from her pocket and offer it to Mister Staunton, the one board member she felt great respect for. He read the letter and handed it to Funston who was closest to him. He then threw up his hands looking at John Fluornoy. 'Well; if someone would offer half again as much salary to Miss Harper, and we were unable to even come close for the next year thanks to the McCann committee, plus stood to lose all our key men as well, I think the *Board* needs some overhauling in its thinking.'

Fluornoy leaned back until his chair squeaked. He was looking almost pleasant. 'I've never doubted your good judgement, Ed,' he said quietly. 'But lately I've had to battle my prejudices right down to the ground to convince myself you weren't becoming mentally scleroid.'

Staunton shrugged. 'Whatever that means,' he growled, and turned, 'Well, Frank,' he said to Belcher, and let Funston finish reading Bonnie's letter before also including him. 'All right, John; what's it going to be: do we stand by our earlier decisions reached in Executive Session to concede some points and stick to others, or do we go over this whole blasted mess again and cause more delay?'

Belcher, Bonnie thought, might have voted for delay, but Funston, looking discouraged, said, 'A new deal, Ed. Nicholson's got to have a new deal. Otherwise we're going to be skinned alive in the press if all these people quit.'

Miss Singleton entered wordlessly, nodded around and lay the completed reports atop John Fluornoy's desk, then just as silently withdrew. Fluornoy gazed at the papers wearing an expression Bonnie would have sworn was veiled triumph, then parcelled out the freshly duplicated copies without a word until he'd finished.

'There are several copies left,' he said amiably – too amiably Bonnie thought – 'I had them in mind for the newspapers. After all, one or two incomplete interviews and some photographs can't possibly explain all that we're doing here at Nicholson.'

Staunton scarcely glanced at his copy of the report although both Funston and Belcher began to avidly read. Staunton seemed to Bonnie to be the most alert, most perceptive member of the governing board. 'Quite a coincidence,' he muttered, 'Miss Singleton bringing the thing at precisely this moment.' He and Fluornoy exchanged glances. Bonnie thought she knew what Staunton was thinking: the Board was being very discreetly blackmailed by Doctor Fluornoy's article. But Staunton didn't mention anything like blackmail at all. What he said was 'John; we simply can't be dictated to by a *woman.*'

That shocked Bonnie. She looked intently at Staunton, her confidence in the man shaken. Before thinking she said with spirit, 'Mister Staunton, would it make any difference if a *man* had made the changes in Ward B?'

Belcher, Funston, Doctor Fluornoy and even Albert Heath were suddenly looking at her. Staunton made a little face. 'Miss Harper, you picked up the wrong intonation. Or perhaps I didn't word it right.

What I meant was that the Board of Governors cannot be dictated to by someone with even less authority than Doctor Fluornoy has.'

'That's not what you said, Mister Staunton.'

John Fluornoy held up a hand. He seemed close to smiling. 'Please, Miss Harper; you've pilloried him properly. I know Ed Staunton too well to think for a moment he has any prejudices against women. We're all a bit on edge here this morning.' Fluornoy, having silenced Bonnie, turned quietly to Staunton. 'All right,' he said. 'The point is, Ed, that the changes *have* been made. I approve of them – belatedly I'll admit – but nevertheless I approve of them. Now the patients are approving, even visiting foreign dignitaries and the press. Nicholson's staff heartily approves. The sensible thing for the governing board to do is also approve. Then we present a united face to the press, to everyone, and it will all end well. I'll be commended as a far-seeing medical practitioner. You, John and Frank will be called progressive visionaries. And the one person who should really get all this praise, Miss Harper, will get a small share – plus a new husband – which isn't really relevant, yet to her it probably is most relevant.'

Belcher scanned the report's pages again looking troubled. He seemed to have lost his initiative somewhere during all this. Funston too, was willing to sit back and let Staunton and Fluornoy battle this out.

But Staunton was a successful business-man, not a fool nor a demagogue; he knew – Bonnie saw it on his face – that what Doctor Fluornoy had said was the precise truth. Still, he got up, stepped to the window, gazed out over the city a moment ordering his thoughts, then swung back.

'John; all right. You and these people of yours have won. Actually, the Board has never really fought you. All it's done was try to understand; evaluate. But I'll tell you two things: one; if this thing doesn't prove practical, we're all going to have to resign. Two; I'm going to insist when the new contracts are drawn up that a clause be inserted making each contract void unless all new innovations are *first* – mind you, *first* – cleared with the Governing Board. Damn it all; this came very close to making Frank, John and me look like fools.'

Doctor Fluornoy arose smiling broadly. Bonnie had never seen such a glowing expression upon his craggy face before. 'You are perfectly correct,' he said to mollify Staunton. He looked straight at Bonnie. 'Isn't he, Miss Harper?'

She nodded, unable to pry the tongue off the roof of her mouth right at that moment.

'And Doctor Heath,' rumbled Fluornoy. 'Do you agree?'

'Perfectly, sir.'

'And you will withdraw your resignation?'

'Yes sir.'

'And you, Miss Harper?'

She finally found her voice. 'I wouldn't really have left Nicholson anyway, gentlemen. But now I'll stay as long as you'll let me.'

The pall was gone, the tension dissipated. Belcher and Funston, still not exactly clear how it had all so suddenly been resolved, vacantly smiled as they also arose.

Staunton exhibited a capacity for quick adjustments by holding up the report. 'I haven't read this thing, Doctor Fluornoy, but I presume it encompasses the ... *our* ... fresh policy at Nicholson.'

'It does, and that's all it does.'

'Then suppose John and Frank and I take it along – those extra copies you mentioned – and give them to the newspapers?'

Fluornoy looked away. Bonnie thought he

might laugh aloud but he didn't. He picked up the extra copies and handed them to Staunton. 'I'd hoped you might do that, Ed.'

It was all over. Staunton weakly smiled at Bonnie. 'About that letter, Miss Harper...'

She stepped to Doctor Fluornoy's wastebasket and dropped the offer from that other hospital into it, stepped back very close to Albert and felt for his fingers. He caught her hand and squeezed, hard.

Staunton nodded, looked at Belcher and Funston and headed for the door. The other board members obediently followed him out of Doctor Fluornoy's office.

CHAPTER TWENTY-TWO

John Fluornoy's concession to outright victory was simply to rub his hands briskly together and look pleasant. 'One thing more,' he said, looking straight at Bonnie. 'McCann...'

She understood perfectly. 'I'll see him straightaway, Doctor Fluornoy. Actually, I suppose I should have suspected he was up to something like that. But he's been so –

243

well – slyly silent the past few days I just didn't think he'd really do anything.'

'He did enough,' exclaimed Fluornoy. 'If you could have been sitting where I was to see those three faces turn sick when it was mentioned the hospital budget wouldn't be increased, you'd have felt like kissing McCann. Apparently, Miss Harper, you have more devoted admirers than you imagine.'

Back in the corridor with Albert, she stepped to a recessed window and looked down over the sprawling city. 'I know exactly what it's like to get a reprieve at the eleventh hour,' she murmured.

Albert's mood was similar to Doctor Fluornoy's mood. 'It's over, the innovations remain, the air is clear again and without doubt you've got a good deal more respect from a board of governors than any other nurse has in this entire dominion.' He took her hand. 'Come along; let's get downstairs.'

When they reached Ward B every eye lifted, every expression was alertly interested, every patient was waiting. Even the nurses, including Helen Cummings, stood expectantly. Bonnie didn't know what to say but Albert did.

'The changes remain and are approved.

Miss Harper stays on as Ward Nurse. The board members are notifying the newspapers of this. There will be quite an article in the evening papers.'

The patients cheered or laughed or hooted, showing in their different ways that they strongly approved. Only Mister McCann sat propped up looking sceptical. Bonnie saw that and walked on over. Albert was suddenly summoned across the way to Ward A and had to leave.

McCann's little shrewd eyes went to Bonnie's face and remained there looking tough and expectant. She said, 'Of course the board had your motion, Mister McCann.'

'And it upset them I'll wager, Miss Harper.'

'It did that, and in their boots I'd have been upset too. Now tell me – it wasn't meant as anything except a threat.'

He didn't hesitate. 'Wedding present, Miss Harper, that's all it was. Of course it was a threat. But on the other hand, if those old fools had persisted...' He acidly smiled and Bonnie saw something just below the surface in Frederick McCann: if he were crossed, or if he were a person's enemy, he would be one of the most thoroughly unrelenting people on earth.

'Will you notify the board your committee has reconsidered, Mister McCann?'

'Aye, girl. The minute I see the evening papers and they've backed you to the hilt.'

She stooped, kissed him swiftly on the cheek and spun to hasten back towards the office. Mister McCann's toughness was in frightful disarray. He looked after her the way a puppy might have looked, then blushed scarlet as the young amputee across the way called over.

'Mister; you've probably got a wife and half-grown kids. If she ever offers to do that again, I'd be enormously obliged if you'd send her over here.'

Several patients laughed. Bonnie heard that in the office and smiled; she thought she knew what it was about.

Doctor Fluornoy came into Ward B shortly before three in the afternoon wearing one of his fresh but baggy white ward-jackets. He made it look still more baggy by walking about with both hands dug deep into each pocket. She met him near the door and reflected that he really didn't look nearly as much like a great old bird of prey about to pounce, as he looked like a gaunt and wise old benign owl.

'Well,' he said, significantly gazing up where McCann was dozing.

She told him what had transpired, even mentioning the kiss. Fluornoy grinned. 'There is an age in men when a young girl's kiss is more precious than all the gold one can imagine. I think you've amply repaid him. Mister Staunton called a few minutes back; he wanted to know if I'd done anything about McCann yet. I shall now call him back and relate that one small kiss broke down all the Chairman's resistance.' He looked down at her. 'Oh yes; I'm to inform you Doctor Heath is waiting downstairs in his auto. Something about looking at furniture. I believe you'll understand.'

She understood but she wanted to somehow show Doctor Fluornoy how much she appreciated *his* part. He *had* swung to her side and he had put his own career on the block for her. Without his backing she'd have been just another unemployed nurse. She stood on tiptoe, placed both hands flat against his chest and kissed him – squarely on the mouth. Then she dropped down, smiled and ran for the office to change into her street clothes.

Old Fluornoy rocked up and down a moment looking round. The Japanese seaman had seen and was grinning. He winked. Doctor Fluornoy gravely winked back, turned and strolled out into the corridor. He whistled a little tune from the Second World War as he hiked for the stairs leading to the third floor. No one believed that was old Fluornoy whistling because never, in all his nearly twelve years as Chief Resident Surgeon at Nicholson, had anyone ever heard him whistle.

Of course the hospital was buzzing with rumours. No one yet knew all the details of that fateful meeting, nor, as a matter of fact, would they know them for several days yet, but that didn't stop the gossipers from starting all manner of wild stories. Mister McCann and one or two others, namely Miss Singleton and perhaps Doctor Fluornoy might have enlightened everyone although it was very improbable John Fluornoy would bother, and as for Althea Singleton, she'd talk when the time was rife simply to set the record straight.

Of course Albert's little announcement in Ward B was scarcely an official statement. Nor had it been very detailed. But for the time being that was all anyone had to build on, so the rumour-mongers took it from there.

As far as Bonnie was concerned the actual details were already becoming *passé;* as she told Albert when they drove away from Nicholson, 'I'm not sure yet whether to laugh or cry.'

He had an appropriate answer. 'Do neither, my love, simply be thankful so many things dovetailed for us. The press, Doctor Fluornoy, the threat from Mc-Cann's committee, the patient and staff reaction – and of course your own courage.'

'You did nothing?' she said, twisting on the car seat.

'Practically nothing, really. It's always been difficult for me to concentrate on three things at once. Being in love, voluntarily altering my entire mode of existence by buying a home and getting married, and worrying about hospital policy and procedure at the same time. Not even to mention having the devil's own time of it keeping my mind off you and on my work.'

She lay her head upon the back of the seat. She'd have put it upon his shoulder except that, being in the bustling heart of the city, it wouldn't have been the proper thing to do. 'Do you know how many more days of freedom are left, Albert?'

He knew and his answer showed how his

mind was working. 'It seems improbable that a man would be straining so hard to *lose* his freedom, love. Here I am with nothing to spend my money on but myself, struggling like a drowning man to get married so I can't do that any more. It doesn't make a whole lot of practical common sense does it?'

'You can still get out.'

'No I can't. I can't even convince myself after over three decades of bachelorhood, being free as an eagle isn't a bad thing.' He grinned at her. 'Terribly entangling, this business of love.'

She smiled. '*Wonderfully* entangling.'

They left the car and went round on foot. Making their purchases was the easiest part, agreeing on them – what type sofa or chair or drapery should go where – was less simple. She finally told him he'd lived as a bachelor too long; that his ideas of interior decoration were all masculine, running to dark leather chairs, sombre drapes, heavy carpeting.

He was indulgent. 'Righto love; from here on you make the selections and I'll just pay the bills.'

But she wouldn't settle for that either. 'It's got to be *mutual*, Albert. This isn't *my* house, it's also yours. I want you to *want* to come home.'

His eyes twinkled. 'Oh; I'll want to do that all right, and what colour the floor coverings are isn't going to influence me too awfully.'

They decided on a different restaurant for their early supper. She chose it and although he went through the procedure with a doubting expression, afterwards he said it had been quite good; that he hadn't eaten any sea food in years and hadn't really expected to like anything so light on one's stomach.

They finally, with dusk settling round-about, decided to drive out to their cottage. He said she really should get home, that the next day was another ten-hour period of labour, and while she agreed with him she still opted for the drive. He did nothing beyond making that one somewhat weak protest, then drove away from the city with a new moon off his left shoulder and the great rolling surf keeping abreast of them past their promontory, past the green fields and shaggy windbreaks of gaunt old slovenly eucalyptus trees.

He had something to tell her but didn't mention it until, leaving the car and walking up their little gravelled path towards the cottage, the time seemed appropriate.

'By the way, I had a little talk with Doctor Fluornoy down on the mezzanine this afternoon while on my way to get the car. He is creating a new post at Nicholson.'

She stepped up on to the porch, turned in curiosity and gazed at him. 'A new post?'

'Administrative Ward Nurse.' At her blank look he explained. 'Supervisor of all Ward Nurses at Nicholson. Sort of administrative assistant to the Chief Surgeon, with what I can best explain as portfolio stature with the Board of Governors.'

'Sounds lofty enough,' she murmured, turning to gaze down across their private world to where distant-breaking surf soundlessly crashed upon a ribbon of snowy beach.

'Oh, it's lofty all right,' he said. 'Think you can handle it?'

She looked at him. He nodded. The pay would be considerably more, he said, the prestige enormous since he was fairly sure no other hospital had a similar post, and the responsibility would be considerable. He finished, summing up by saying, 'It's your wedding present from Doctor Fluornoy. He told me that. He also asked me to tell you tonight.'

'Why wouldn't *he* tell me, Albert?'

'I think it's because, despite his crustiness, Doctor Fluornoy embarrasses easily. He was afraid you might jump up and kiss him or something like that. Very irregular you know.'

She laughed. 'But I *did* kiss him, just before I left Ward B this afternoon.'

'Did he faint?'

'No. He looked a little red, but I didn't wait to see what else happened; I was a little embarrassed myself.'

Albert stepped over, slid an arm round her waist and stood close gazing out over their still and silent world. 'Perhaps in the future if you confined yourself just to kissing your husband…?'

She turned in his arms, slowly raised both arms, placed them around his shoulders and drew him still closer. 'Forever,' she whispered. 'Forever, Albert.'

A bird called from a tree out back. It got an answer farther off. Frogs cheerily croaked in the rank grass where they'd run the sprinkler. The little new moon, giving practically no light at all, moved a few degrees and diluted some of the shadows where the lovers stood in soft rapture, and all that foaming surf finally sent a soft drumroll of sound up as far as their cottage.

'Forever,' he whispered. 'Bonnie; I'd no idea it would be so – well – so all-permeating.'

'That's what true love really is all about, Albert.'

'Wisely said,' he murmured, and sought her lips again. That time the moon lost its tenuous grip on the shadows and they closed round the clinging shapes.

This Large Print Book for the partially sighted, who cannot read normal print, is published under the auspices of

THE ULVERSCROFT FOUNDATION